AN ACCIDENT WAITING TO DRAGON

BRIMSTONE INC.

ABIGAIL OWEN

AN INFERNO RISING & FIRE'S EDGE CROSSOVER NOVELLA

This is a work of fiction. Names, characters, places, and incidents are either the product of the author's imagination or are used fictitiously, and any resemblance to actual persons living or dead, business establishments, events, or locales, is entirely coincidental.

An Accident Waiting to Dragon

COPYRIGHT © 2024 by Author Abigail Owen

Blue Violet Publishing, LLC

All rights reserved. No part of this book may be used or reproduced in any manner whatsoever without written permission of the author except in the case of brief quotations embodied in critical articles or reviews.

Cover Art by *Blue Violet Publishing, LLC*

DEDICATION

To all my fellow book dragons out there!

AN ACCIDENT WAITING TO DRAGON

A BRIMSTONE INC. NOVELLA

An Inferno Rising & Fire's Edge
dragon shifter crossover novella...

It's not the heat...it's the pixie dust.

The day her brother died, Gwendolyn Moonsoar fled from her veil of pixies. Grief drove her away, but a broken heart made her stay gone for good. Lucky for Gwen, Brimstone Inc. was there to break her fall. Now, as a special courier transporting the most valuable and dangerous items of the supernatural world, Gwen is good at her job. Damn good. After all, disappearing is her specialty.

DRAGON SHIFTER ASHER KATO will always be haunted by his best friend Goran's death. Although a promise he made gave him no choice, Asher will never forgive himself for the role he played...or the fallout it caused with Goran's younger sister, Gwen. Burying himself in his role as second-in-command of the blue dragons is his only escape. Unfortunately, the peace they fought so hard for isn't meant for a warrior like him. So, when a courier transporting a rare basilisk egg goes missing, Asher volunteers to track them down.

Except Asher's mission ends up stranding him on a deserted island with the only woman he's ever wanted....a pixie who would rather vanish forever than spend a single second with him.

CONTENT / TRIGGER WARNING

I write addictive, action-packed romantasy and paranormal romance stories. These books may include elements that might not be suitable for all readers, including but not limited to: violence, gore, death, explicit sexual content, swearing, supernatural or magical themes, and an irreverent sense of humor. It is my hope and personal goal that all elements have been handled sensitively and in an age-appropriate manner. I trust you to know your own age, experiences, beliefs, values, triggers and limits. Read at your own discretion.

Please take note and take care, and get ready for a helluva ride!

UNDER 18: *Get permission from your parent or guardian to read my books.*

PROLOGUE

ASHER

Thirteen years ago...

Dragon steel shackles kept Asher from moving, let alone shifting—fuck. If he tried, he'd be cleaved in two.

Whoever had taken him had also covered his head in a hood, leaving only his senses of sound and smell to help him adjust. Smell not as much because the hood smelled like ball sweat and mold. Godsdamn it.

They hadn't gone far. That much he sensed.

Best guess, they were in a remote glen somewhere near Ben Nevis, the Scottish mountain stronghold of the blue dragon shifters, which meant whoever grabbed him from his bed inside the mountain didn't want everyone seeing what happened next.

He was so fucked.

A year as a spy in that mountain, pretending to be one of the corrupt King Thanatos's loyal bodyguards and warriors, and he'd thought he'd covered his tracks, that he'd earned the king's respect. How had he been caught? Or…was this a different enemy of Thanatos's coming after one of his leaders?

Either was possible.

With a deep, unpleasant breath, Asher controlled his heartbeat through sheer will and training and remained still as he was carried farther and farther by hands, not talons. Walking, not flying.

They stopped, and even the breeze went still, the birds silent in the trees.

Then, with a tug, his hood came off and Asher blinked, his dragon shifter eyes adjusting easily to the forest darkness.

A new moon. No light to help him see.

Not that he needed it. Asher's captor stood behind him, but he didn't look back. Because only a few yards in front of him, also on his knees and bound in dragon steel, was…

Goran Woodshield.

The sight of his best friend's dead serious face was like a gut punch, and it took everything in Asher to control his reaction.

Goran's presence here answered all Asher's questions.

His friend had been acting as Asher's scout and go-between to get the information he gathered to Ladon Ormarr, the man fighting to usurp the throne. Asher and Goran had been friends since childhood. Long fucking time for dragons. For pixies, too.

This wasn't Thanatos's enemies.

This was Thanatos.

He'd come for Asher's head. Goran's too. That was a bigger problem because Goran had been waiting for this moment to die.

How do I get us out of this?

Taking in the wooded clearing, Asher tried to think. He couldn't shift. Dragon steel was the only thing that could hold a dragon shifter, so that was out. What else? Goran was a wood pixie and didn't have to have his hands free to use his power. Only, thanks to his heightened senses, Asher knew more than a few dragons lurked in the woods around them. He and Goran might be able to bust their way out, but they'd never make it far.

As if Goran had followed Asher's train of thought, he gave the tiniest shake of his head.

Not a warning.

A refusal.

He wasn't going to try to escape.

Asher's heart dropped like a boulder to the bottom of his stomach. He knew what was coming. What Goran was going to do. The sacrifice he was planning to make.

They'd agreed on this plan. Or, more accurately, Goran had essentially forced Asher's hand with a blood oath made through magic and bloodshed. He'd trusted Goran, swearing blindly before he knew what his friend was going to ask of him. Now he wished he hadn't trusted so easily.

Because the possible scenario Goran had planned for, even been waiting for, was happening. Now.

Heart growing heavier by the second, Asher stared hard at Goran. Tall for a pixie, Goran's face was a triangle with a pointed, stubborn-as-hells chin. His coloring he'd gotten from his father—a pixie who'd basically been a second father to Asher—light brown hair, hazel eyes, and, of all things, freckles.

As familiar to Asher as his own face. How was he supposed to kill Goran?

Don't make me do this. Please, he silently begged Goran.

But the only way to salvage this was making Thanatos

believe that Goran was the spy, not Asher. They both knew the king, knew the only act that would convince him of Asher's loyalty was this. Him killing Goran.

And a slowly dying man was a desperate man. Already Goran's lips and ears were starting to turn black with the disease slowly ravaging his body. A fact he'd hidden from everyone but Asher—including Goran's own family, and his sister Gwen. Instead of fading away slowly, he had wanted to make his end count. This was *his* choice.

But it had only been a contingency plan, damn it.

They were never supposed to end up here.

"Asher Kato." A voice like smoke came out of the darkness a beat before Thanatos himself stepped into Asher's line of sight. "Member of my King's Guard. My best warrior. I was thinking of appointing you as my Viceroy of Defense." A muscle twitched in the side of the king's jaw. "The only question I have for you is…how will you choose to die?"

Asher only had a split second to decide what to do.

The surety, the will to see this through, glittered in his friend's eyes. Asher didn't need his dragon's telepathy to know that Goran was silently urging him to take this final step with him.

Fuck.

This was happening.

They were doing this. His stomach curled, souring, and turning to sludge. He gave the slightest shake of his head, one that asked Goran to stop. Not to make him do this.

Not to force his hand.

Goran tipped his chin just enough for Asher to get the message. There was no other choice. Ladon needed Asher to stay where he was, providing invaluable information. Goran was right.

I will go to the seventh hell for this.

Gwen would *never* forgive him for this.

But the decision was made. The blood oath between them had made sure of that.

Time to put on a show.

"I know this man," Asher started. And had the satisfaction of seeing Thanatos pause. The king hadn't been expecting that admission. "Why is he here?"

Thanatos swung his piercing blue gaze from Goran to Asher, tipping his head to study him closely. "You admit you know him?"

"Yes."

Thanatos's lips compressed. He'd never really liked Asher's tendency to brevity. "He's a friend?"

"Yes."

Across the way, Goran grunted. Pixie for irritation. In other words, start talking.

Asher unclenched his jaw. "We grew up together, north of here, near my home." In a smaller dragon mountain near Goran's flutter of pixies.

Thanatos rocked back on his heels, taking that in. "Then what the hells was he doing skulking through our mountain with papers containing information about our coffers? Was he there to visit you?"

Yes. But the information Goran had carried was too damning to admit it. "No. I have no clue why he was there." He forced fire to reflect in his eyes. "What did you do, Goran?"

Goran glared at Asher like he wanted to rip his throat out, playing his part. "I did what you should have done all along."

Asher curled his lip in a snarl.

And Thanatos drew his shoulders back. "He was bringing information from a spy and traitor in my mountain to Ladon Ormarr."

Asher snarled at Goran, straining against his shackles.

"Are you in league with that godsdamned traitor?"

Goran's lips tipped in a characteristic lopsided grin, like he didn't have a care in the world. "To eradicate this asshole?" He nodded at Thanatos. "Yeah."

"You were my *friend*," Asher said, his voice turning raw with the undeniability of exactly what was about to happen.

Goran's shrug held no mercy and no regret. "Then you should have listened to me when I told you to get out of Ben Nevis. You're going to have to kill me to stop me now, brother."

Brother. Asher had hoped that maybe Goran would become that not just in words.

"Well, well… This is a turn of events I did not foresee," Thanatos murmured, crossing his arms as he took in the scene.

And from the glint in his eyes, he didn't believe it, either.

He moved to stand before Asher, producing a key from his pocket. And with each click of a lock, each release of one of the bindings, more blue dragons in their human forms stepped out of the darkness and into the clearing. Thanatos's lackies. Witnesses.

Or killers, if Asher and Goran tried to run.

"You want to prove yourself loyal to me?" Thanatos asked in a low voice. "Execute this man. Here and now." This was it.

No choice.

There is no other choice.

Asher's dragon, warily silent until this moment, gave a small huffing whine.

But he didn't dare allow the emotion to show on his face. Not for a second.

Closing his eyes, Asher took a deep breath, and called forth the dragon from within, shifting and giving the animal side of him control. In a silent rush, his body changed. His soul stayed in place as his physical form shifted around his essence—everything human about him, including his clothes, absorbed into his new shape. The trees flew past as his perspective rose, higher and higher, until he towered above, his deep navy scales closer to black in the darkness.

As he shifted, Asher's senses sharpened, his sight able to pick up the rapid pulse at Goran's neck. His friend wasn't as brave as he was letting on.

Who would be when facing death by dragon fire?

Bile churned in Asher's stomach, mixing toxically with fire, while he looked his friend in the eyes, never looking away, trying to...

He didn't even know what.

Offer some sort of comfort? Be there for him? Soak in these last moments of Goran's life? Come up with some desperate last-ditch attempt to fix this a different way? To flee? To take his friend and run?

He was a seasoned, hardened warrior. He'd gutted opponents. He'd ordered his own men into battle and fought beside them every step of the way. Violence and bloodshed were a part of his life, and he'd never once flinched from it. But now...

Every part of him was protesting so brutally, he had to clamp down hard on his muscles to keep from visibly shaking, to keep from vomiting.

The first words Goran had said to him rattled around in Asher's head. *"Want to see what I can do?"*

Goran had found him tucked between rocks on the side of the mountain the day his parents had died, when Asher had realized he had no one. Despite his illustrious blood lines, he'd had no family, no friends. He'd been a loner. So had his parents.

Goran hadn't asked questions, hadn't tried to cajole. Instead he'd ignored the tears on Asher's face, focusing instead on using his magic to grow a tree where none had been before.

He'd only been six years old.

They'd been inseparable after that.

And then there was Gwen...

"You can't do it, can you?" Goran taunted now. "I always knew you were a coward."

Asher growled deep in his throat. A warning. At the same time, he sent his friend a single thought. *"I will take care of them for you."*

Goran's family. Especially Gwen.

If she ever forgave him...

Eyes glittering with what might be tears but looked like anger, Goran sneered. "Come on," the challenge rang through the clearing.

His friend was ready for this death. Asking for it. Begging even.

Without warning, his friend lashed out with all the power a wood pixie could muster. Roots of trees burst from the ground, twining together to form a massive sword. He slammed it down on Asher's back, striking his tail.

Agony ripped through Asher in a searing trail which threatened to obliterate him right there.

Blue flames erupted from his maw on a roar of fury and pain and regret, hitting Goran dead on.

Asher held the fire for longer than he had to. Held it even as his body wavered, swaying like a reed in a hurricane as his own injury shrieked at him. He held it until the trees all around them exploded in flames, and the men watching had to shift themselves to be safe from the conflagration.

The fire cut off abruptly as Asher swayed wildly, then the world tipped over sideways.

The last thing he saw was the pile of ashes on the ground.

Ashes that only seconds ago had been his best friend.

CHAPTER ONE

ASHER

Present day...

As far as Asher was concerned, there was nothing more teeth grindingly frustrating than sitting in a conference room, choked by the fancy suit and tie he'd been forced to wear. He listened intently to another unending debate the bureaucratic types were currently having about the state of dragon shifter kind. Problems that seemed small after five-hundred years of fighting.

But the war was over, the corrupt kings removed, and new leaders installed. And, with the rise of the phoenix, they had peace at last.

Which basically puts me out of a fucking job.

Not really. His position as beta of the blue dragons made him second-in-command and next in line to rule, at least until Ladon and Skylar Ormarr—the Blue Clan's king and queen—spawned little fire breathers of their own. Problem was, Asher was a warrior, not a diplomat. Talking—unless it involved giving orders—wasn't exactly his thing.

His dragon huffed in agreement. The animal side of him hated this as much as he did.

The oval shaped table sat fifteen dragon shifters and at least another ten lined the walls in more chairs. And they had yet to settle a single issue. Pussy footing around feelings and playing politics like a chessboard...even a mate by his side wouldn't make this shit tolerable.

Not that he'd ever have a mate.

He'd lost his chance the day he'd killed Goran.

He just hadn't known it until later. Until he'd told Gwen...

An image crowded into his head of delicate lines—a face with a slightly pointed chin, freckled-dusted button nose, and golden eyes that had last looked at him as if he'd turned into a monster.

Now that the war was over, maybe the time had finally come to find her and...

And what? Remind her of all the reasons she should hate him?

The blood oath he'd taken meant he couldn't tell her anything about her brother's role as a spy or about his death, including the fact that Asher had sworn the oath to Goran at all. He'd spent the last thirteen years trying to think of any way around it. "We need more resources." Ladon growled at the woman sitting at the head of the table, blue eyes flaring with fire.

Jerked back to the discussion, Asher ruthlessly cut off any thought of Gwen.

In that tone of voice and with the glower on Ladon's face,

most would cower from the man whose nickname was the "Blood King." But Asher held his relaxed posture, leaning back in his seat and keeping his expression deliberately blank.

To give her credit, Luu Meilin, Queen of the Green Dragons, not only didn't flinch at Ladon's glare, but she returned it with one of her own, a small warning growl crawling up her throat.

"We mean no disrespect." Skylar elbowed Ladon who, after an aggrieved glance at his mate, crossed his arms, his expression mulish.

Skylar rolled her eyes. "The riches of the dragon shifters primarily ended up in the coffers of the Red, White, and Green clans. Stolen from the Black, Gold, and Blue clans."

"We all agree with this," Meilin said, still glaring at Ladon.

"Well…" Skylar spread her hands wide in appeal. "What's been returned to us so far is hardly a drop in the bucket. We need to be able to support our people—"

Meilin slashed an impatient hand through the air, cutting Skylar off. "I don't know any other way to tell you that *we* don't have it. I'm not hoarding. I'm not hiding the riches. It's *not here.*"

"Then where the fuck is it?" Ladon snarled.

This time two of Meilin's personal guard stepped forward, flanking their new ruler's chair. A warning.

Meilin waved them off.

"You promised to handle this diplomatically," Skylar softly reminded her mate under her breath.

Several shifters around the table chuckled—all their hearing was enhanced, so no one close would have missed it. A rare spurt of humor shot through Asher, not that he smiled.

Instead, he studied the newly voted in queen.

The only child of the recently executed King Fraener—a greedy, corrupt horror of a leader just like Thanatos had once been—Meilin was the first dragon queen in history. Ladon and Skylar and their allies were waiting to see if Meilin would turn out to be cut from a different cloth than her father.

So far, Asher was impressed.

The door to the conference room suddenly opened, making all the shifters at the table tense and turn toward the possible threat. Peace may have come to dragons at last, but the war had been recent enough that no one was relaxed yet.

Too soon.

Asher didn't so much as twitch, even with his back to the door. He'd heard the tread of the person coming down the hall while everyone else was apparently distracted by the ongoing argument. He'd also recognized the patter—one of Meilin's personal assistants—no need for concern.

"My apologies." The younger male dragon shifter, probably too young to have had his first shift, a cousin perhaps, bowed at the waist to his queen, then the room in general.

Meilin beckoned him over, but he didn't bother to whisper in her ear. In a room this small and quiet and full of shifters, there was no point. "Someone named Delilah, with Brimstone Inc., would like an audience, my queen. She says it urgent."

After a single blink, Meilin straightened in her chair. "Clear the room please."

Interest piqued, Asher's dragon lifted its head inside him. But Asher didn't move to comply, instead waiting for his king and queen to decide what to do first.

Skylar's eyebrows shot straight up while Ladon's bunched in a frown. "Seriously—"

Meilin held up a hand, staying Ladon's words. "You two

should stay, along with your beta." She flicked a glance in Asher's direction.

"My queen?" the man to Meilin's right murmured in a thick Australian accent—Asher couldn't remember the guy's name—her Viceroy of the Reserve.

"Stay, Hank," she said. "You too, Kasem."

The guard to her right pulled his shoulders back with a sharp nod.

Meilin waited for everyone else to file out, leaving the room feeling empty after being stuffed for hours. Even so, she waited for the sounds of steps to recede before she nodded at her assistant.

Immediately, the younger man grabbed a handheld console from the table, typing away. A minute later, they were connected by video call. Delilah Blakesly stared back at them from the screen, professional in a pristine white suit with her raven hair gathered back elegantly. Her jade green eyes didn't so much as glint. The woman was as coolly collected, as always. The owner and operator of Brimstone Inc., a company that provided myriad services to the supernaturally inclined, Delilah was mysterious in that no one knew exactly what she was or what her powers were. But she'd helped Asher's people many ways in the past—big and small—and Ladon and Skylar both trusted her.

So, Asher trusted her too.

Apparently, so did his dragon. Not a single growl.

"What happened?" Meilin asked, not bothering to fill the rest of them in on what this was about in the first place.

"My courier has disappeared."

Courier? He slid a glance to the green queen. What important item did she need Delilah's courier for?

"Where?" Meilin prompted.

Delilah waved a hand, and the screen immediately changed to show a map with a small red dot moving across

17

Australia. It was headed north. Then it stopped. No more blipping dot.

"I have a tracer on her," Delilah told them. "Last contact was just south of Darwin, fifty-two minutes ago."

Ladon leaned forward. "What is she delivering?"

Delilah paused infinitesimally, glancing toward Meilin as if checking for permission to share that detail. "A rainbow basilisk egg."

Interesting.

"Aren't those incredibly rare?" Skylar asked Ladon.

Ladon only nodded.

But Delilah heard her. "Yes, they are. Rainbow basilisks are coveted for multiple benefits—healing, future telling, and so forth. It was found by one of the green dragon colonies in Australia."

"Why bring it to dragons and not basilisks?" Skylar asked.

"Basilisks need dragon fire to hatch." Delilah hesitated a tiny moment.

And Meilin was the closest dragon leader, which explained why it was being brought here.

Delilah cleared her throat. "The last known rainbow basilisk hatched at the end of the Great Darkness that enveloped the world."

Seven hells.

Asher hadn't been alive for that. Dragon shifters lived almost two thousand years, but that had been long before even the oldest dragon now alive could remember. A war of creatures of darkness against those who wielded light. "Are you saying that's what we're headed for?" Ladon asked, words clipped. "Another Great Darkness?"

Delilah spread her hands in a gesture that indicated even she wasn't sure. Which was saying a lot. The woman seemed to know everything.

"What do we know about the courier?" Meilin demanded.

With a slight nod, Delilah expanded. "We know she secured the egg from your colony. She checked in with me before starting out. They've confirmed she left unhindered with no sign of danger."

"Have you sent someone after her?" Meilin asked.

Delilah linked her fingers together. "That's why I'm contacting you. She's the best at what she does. If her signal went out, it's either because she's dead or, the more likely scenario, because she wanted it to. A signal to me that she's in trouble."

"What's the protocol?" Asher asked.

"She can ditch the egg and run, or she goes incognito, acting as a human. I have certain signs to look for to tell me where she is."

"Which is more likely?"

"She'll exhaust all options to finish the job before she ditches the egg."

Impressive. But not unusual if Delilah hired this woman.

"Is the egg that important?" Skylar asked.

"To me? No. My courier is the priority, but she might think differently..." Delilah shrugged. "I called to ask for your help. I'd like to send help in her direction. As soon as I see her signal, I can give specifics."

"I'll go." The words were out of Asher's mouth before he made a conscious decision to step up and volunteer. Ladon and Skylar both did a double take.

"Really?" Ladon asked in a low aside. "Why?"

Asher's dragon unfurled in him, interest fully caught now. A mission. That's what they needed.

He said nothing, and Ladon didn't push it.

Kasem scowled. "We have our own trackers here—"

"No one is as good as Asher," Ladon interrupted.

"With respect," Skylar tacked on for her mate, whose jaw tensed.

The queen's lead guard wasn't letting it go. "This is—"

Meilin rose gracefully from the table, silencing Kasem. "Asher's reputation is well known. He'll go, with his king and queen's permission. All I ask is that he reports to me as well. Directly."

Ladon glanced at Skylar, who nodded, then at Asher, passing on the nod.

Asher barely kept from rubbing his hands together in anticipation, his dragon stretching, already ready to go. Finally something he could use his skills for.

On the screen, Delilah also nodded. "I suggest you start in Darwin and head north. She'll try to take the shortest route but may have to lay some false tracks."

He'd already decided on that as a first step. "Tell me more about your courier."

"She's a moon pixie. She can travel by and hide in moonlight. Very useful."

Asher froze halfway out of his seat.

"Wow." Kasem's murmur vaguely penetrated the sudden roar in Asher's ears. Instant, bone-deep knowledge struck him in the chest, and for the first time in a long time, he had to focus to leash down his dragon.

There was only one pixie that could be.

"No wonder she's good," Kasem said. "Who is she?"

Delilah's smile was enigmatic. "Her name is—"

"Gwen Moonsoar," Asher said.

Delilah's gaze narrowed on him sharply. "How would you know that?"

Which confirmed it.

Fuck. Of course, it's Gwen.

It's like his memories only moments ago had summoned her. More came at him hard and fast now—of silky black hair and laughing pale gold eyes, of lips tipped in a sweet smile or pursed in irritation. Did she still taste as sweet? Did she laugh like she used to? Did she still hate him?

It was a damn good thing he'd already volunteered, because they'd have to kill him now to stop him from going after her.

CHAPTER TWO

Gwen

Being hunted was a pain in the ass.

The single prop SeaRey plane cut through crystal blue skies. Gwen had bought it outright with a portion of the cash Delilah always provided for jobs "just in case things went sideways." This wasn't the first time that had come in handy.

She wasn't sure yet what was hunting her.

Whatever it was moved in darkness. Her magical instincts had told her that much in the middle of the rain forest just south of Darwin. It could've been a creature that lived in those trees, but given what Gwen was carrying, that was less likely.

Transporting rare, valuable, and even dangerous items was Gwen's job—and the rare egg definitely counted as all three. Delilah gave Gwen the tough assignments for a reason. She was good at her job. Damn good. After all, pixies were mysterious by nature, only being seen when they wanted. But disappearing...that was Gwen's specialty.

She'd made it to the city without an encounter, and then spent several days there hiding and figuring out her next move.

Now here she was, flying over Indonesia.

The amphibian aircraft was on the older side, which meant it could set down on both water and land. It wasn't the prettiest thing in the world, but the previous owners had certainly taken good care of the engines and moving parts, and that's all Gwen cared about. She glanced at the pack strapped in the seat beside her, the basilisk egg wrapped up nice and tight.

Everything under control. For now. How long that lasted was anyone's guess.

All she had to do was make it to a small airstrip on East Nusa Tenggara, an island in Indonesia. If she could land there before dark, she was golden, thanks to a colony of jinn she was friendly with in the area. They owed her a favor. Most of the creatures that went bump in the night weren't stupid enough to go against a whole colony of jinn.

Pretending to be human and traveling by plane, even logging a flight path, was essentially a flare she'd sent up for Delilah to send help.

"Hopefully that doesn't bite me in the ass," she muttered to herself.

It was possible whatever was after the egg could find that information and get to her faster. Hopefully whatever, or whoever, her boss sent would find her somewhere along the route before then. Maybe even by tomorrow.

After that...

The plane eddied with a small crosscurrent of air, and she automatically corrected. She didn't think much of it, probably an upper coming off the summer heat of one of the islands below.

Gwen raised her gaze from the plane's instruments across a calm sea of deep blue dotted here and there with tufts of green or sometimes black or sandy colored rock. While some parts of Indonesia were struggling with overpopulation, more of the islands that made up the nation were unsettled, with many uninhabited islands scattered across the Southeast Asian seas.

Another eddy and she corrected again.

By the fourth or fifth time the plane tried to slip sideways or drop with turbulence, Gwen frowned, scanning the skies in front of her for any sign of incoming weather. Nothing. A perfect, clear, sunny day.

Another shake hit her, harder this time, and Gwen maneuvered the controls to turn the plane in a lazy looping circle to see behind her. She'd barely started her turn when she clocked the weather hurtling toward her. The ominous line of dark, angry clouds rose thousands of feet into the air like a giant tsunami.

"Son of a bitch," Gwen snarled.

She completed the rest of her turn, and as soon as she leveled out, she increased her speed, pushing the little plane faster than she should. The last thing she needed was to still be in the air when that struck. She was only a halfway decent pilot, mostly because she rarely traveled by anything but her own wings and moonlight. Unfortunately, she wasn't close enough to an island to set down yet.

She centered the closest one in her line of sight, but no matter how long she flew, land didn't seem to get much closer on the horizon. The longer she stayed in the air, the stronger the winds became, whipping at her little plane—dropping it, raising it, knocking it from side to side—until the poor thing was groaning at her in violent protest.

"We're close. Not too much farther," she coaxed, tempted to give it a comforting pat.

She'd only turned around one other time to check how close the storm was, but after that, she hadn't bothered. This was clearly no ordinary storm. Her plane should be able to stay ahead of it, and yet it was bearing down on her rapidly. Best guess was a supernatural reason.

Mental note...the next plane I buy needs to come with rear view mirrors or a backward facing camera.

The daylight had gradually been dimming as the weather approached, but suddenly the sun disappeared. The clouds had to be right on top of her. She leaned forward, looking up. Sure enough, she could see the edges coming over the top of her like teeth in the mouth of a giant, like the storm was trying to swallow her.

She needed to set down. Now. She could land on the water, but she'd need a cove for protection. What she couldn't do was fly on her own pixie steam between islands after the storm passed. It was too far, so she needed her plane intact.

Suddenly, the little plane stopped all forward momentum, as if a giant fist of storm-driven darkness had grabbed her by the tail and held on. The plane sputtered, trying hard to keep going, but the winds had shifted, coming at her from the nose. Before Gwen could do anything, shadow suddenly consumed her small aircraft.

Not the storm.

Shadow.

"Holy shit," she muttered.

But it wasn't that, or the rattling and shaking of the aircraft, that sent her heart into her throat. It was the figure of darkness, floating directly in front of her.

A wraith.

That's what was after her? The death dealers were rare, even more secretive than pixies, and damn hard to escape.

Adrenaline pumping, searing her skin, she stared, and it stared right back.

The creature floating just ahead of her plane reminded her of the human depiction of reapers—the black cloak hood pulled over so she couldn't see its face, tattered at the sleeves and the bottom. No feet though. Wraiths didn't have bodies the way humans did, the way pixies did. They were physical and could be injured, but at the same time, they were just… darkness. She didn't try to reason with how they worked. They just did.

She swore the damn thing smiled at her though.

Did wraiths have teeth? She'd never really thought about it.

The thing shot forward, straight for her, and no glass windscreen was gonna keep it out. It could pass right through anything clear like that, the same way shadow did.

Pure instinct had Gwen shoving the stick straight forward, putting the plane into a sharp dive. A hand of shadow passed in front of her face as if the wraith reached for her but missed. Keeping an eye on the altimeter, she didn't pull up. She probably couldn't outrun it, but she could damn well try.

Any second now she'd get to the bottom of the clouds and be able to see where the water was. Right?

She found herself leaning forward like that would help her see it sooner.

The needle turned over, inching down faster than she liked as she blew through thousands of feet. It was a miracle the plane hadn't stalled yet.

If I don't see anything but cloud by two thousand feet, I'm pulling up.

Actually, that was probably foolish too. These islands

were mountainous and could reach heights between six and twelve thousand feet. What if she flew right into one?

Gwen held herself tightly, like she was bracing for the impact coming at her any second.

I'll probably be dead before I know what happened.

Not exactly a consolation.

She was probably dead anyway because the second she landed or crashed, whichever came first, the wraith would have her.

Suddenly, she burst out from under the clouds which blotted out the sun so that it was like night had fallen. But at least she could see in front of her. A movement out the side window caught her eye, and she jerked her gaze that direction just in time to see the wraith coming straight for her.

Damn that thing moved fast. Bat out of hell didn't even begin to cover it.

Gwen forced herself to sit still, intending to wait until it got close enough before she flipped the plane and hopefully outmaneuvered it.

She gripped the stick harder, ready to react.

Then, just as her tension reached fever pitch, a flicker of shadow overhead dimmed the cockpit half a beat before something massive slammed into the wraith from above.

CHAPTER THREE

Gwen

The thing that took out the wraith, dragging it down and out of her sight, was so big it kept going by her window in an undulating current of scales.

A dragon.

Meilin had to have sent help. The sharp burst of relief in her chest was all she had time to feel about that. This wasn't over.

If they're going down, I'm going up.

She pulled back on the stick, climbing as fast as the little plane could against the drag of the stormy winds. Rain kicked in as she went, the sound loudly pelting the body of the plane.

Suddenly, the wraith appeared off to her right, and she had enough time to shiver as she locked eyes with the eyeless sockets fixated on her before the dragon scooped up from below, snapping it in deadly jaws.

Only the wraith turned to mist before the dragon could sink in enough to hold it. The dragon's ribs expanded, the blue glow of dragon fire peeping through the cracks between scales stretched wide. Shock pelted her harder than the storm raging outside as dark blue fire blasted from its maw, lighting up the skies and giving the wraith no choice but to flee, and the dragon followed.

Wait. Blue. Navy blue.

She *knew* this dragon.

A white-hot dagger of anger and confusion sliced through her, leaving a blazing trail of resentment behind. She'd never wanted to see Asher Kato again as long as she lived.

What the fuck is he doing here?

That thought barely registered when, with a blinding flash, lightning struck her plane dead on, the simultaneous crack of thunder sending her ears ringing. In theory, the Faraday cage design would keep her safe inside while the current travelled through the body of the plane and out the tail, leaving the plane unharmed. Instead, every circuit in the plane fritzed out, taking with it the screens and panels of her instruments. At the same time, she was thrown against the door as the craft spun straight down.

The prop must've locked up.

"No, no, no, no," she chanted, trying not to hear the panic in her own voice.

Gwen wasted precious seconds trying to get things to restart, the G-forces swinging the plane round and round pressing her into her seat and the side of the door. Blood rushed to her extremities, abandoning her head, tunneling her vision.

"Good thing I have wings," she muttered as she struggled to reach for the basilisk egg.

She managed to get it strapped to her back, impossible to

dislodge if the wraith or the dragon got too close to her, or heaven forbid another lightning strike came her way again. Even she couldn't be that unlucky twice, could she?

Time to abandon ship…or plane.

She tugged at the door handle, then tugged again. "Shit."

Even magical pixies couldn't fight the natural world sometimes. She couldn't get the door open. Shouldering it until she bruised herself didn't work, and she only had another minute or two before she crashed, not that she could see the ground through the now blinding storm.

Gwen managed to turn in her seat and try to kick the door. The thing only budged a little before it slammed back against her.

Right. New plan.

"Next time, Gwen, land *when* you see the clouds," she grumbled at herself as she climbed, hand over fist, dragging herself awkwardly between the two seats toward the other door. Fighting against the invisible hand of physics pushing her back toward her own side slowed her progress to a crawl.

She was almost there when suddenly the plane jerked to halt so abruptly, she was thrown the rest of the way, smacking her cheek hard enough to see stars. In the next second, the roof of the plane was ripped right off, like she was being peeled out of a sardine can. Rain bombarded her through the jagged hole only to stop when a giant blue dragon eye covered the gap, staring in at her.

"What are you doing?" Asher's voice boomed inside her head. *"Get out of there."*

She'd never thought she'd hear those dark, rough tones again in her lifetime, except in the dreams of him that haunted her almost every night.

Something about that shot ire through her stronger than the damned lightning bolt and just as sizzling.

"I'm taking a nap," she snapped back. "What do you think?"

Scrambling as fast as she could, she climbed out of the hole he'd made for her as he held them aloft, massive wings beating at the air methodically, sounding like an umbrella in the storm. "Where's the wraith?" she asked.

"Damned if I know," he growled as she climbed up his side to his neck, right at the apex that met his shoulders, situating herself between two nasty looking spikes. *"Pretty sure I caught him with fire, but that doesn't mean he's gone."*

Nothing survived a direct hit of dragon fire, except dragons, and even then, sometimes they also succumbed. She'd seen the remains of her brother after he'd died that way. Assuming Asher had hit the wraith dead on, they should be safe. Even if he didn't...fire and light were the two things a wraith hated most in the world.

They could deal with it.

The storm was a different matter.

Asher tossed the plane away from them like it was nothing more than a child's toy and took off into the skies. Gwen didn't exactly hold on for dear life, but it was a close thing. Dragons flew so much faster than pixies. The wind grabbed at her from all directions. The storm tore at her like it was trying to peel her off his back the way he'd peeled the roof off her plane. She couldn't see a damn thing.

"Be careful," she yelled into the chaos. "I don't think this is a normal storm. Something else is wielding it."

"I know."

"Just trying to help," she huffed under her breath. "See if I bother next time."

Not that there would be a next time if she could help it.

Once upon a blissfully naïve time, she'd been so head over heels in love with Asher Kato she couldn't have said which way was up. She'd idolized him. Hero-worshipped him even.

And just when he'd started to look at her differently, like she wasn't just his best friend's kid sister…

Well… that was before Goran died.

This was now.

With zero warning, the wraith suddenly reappeared, wrapping its arms around her and jerking her off Asher's back so fast Gwen yelped.

Below her, she could see Asher start to wheel around. Only once they were clear of him, lightning blasted through his right wing.

"Asher!" she shrieked.

The immense, navy-colored dragon roared as electricity danced over his body, tracing the lines of his bones and spine all the way down to the mangled tail he'd clearly lost half of since the last time she'd seen him. He seized and then went limp, plummeting from the sky, his huge body wheeling around his one good wing the same way she'd been spinning in her plane only a few moments ago.

Gwen's entire body went cold with fear.

The yell that ripped from Gwen's throat came from someplace primal. Without thinking, her body exploded, moonlight pouring from her skin like a star going supernova. Even if they'd been in daylight, anything looking at her would no longer see her features, her form obliterated by brilliant radiance.

She thought, maybe, that she heard the wraith scream.

In any case, it definitely let her go. Instead of opening her wings, Gwen dropped toward the earth as she aimed her body like an arrow, shooting down headfirst with her legs stuck straight out behind her and her arms tucked in close to her sides. She didn't have to look hard to spot Asher, who was still falling out of control. She aimed for him.

If he was conscious, he wouldn't shift. She knew he

wouldn't. His larger form could take the impact better than his human form.

But is he conscious?

She didn't think so.

Eyes watering, she squinted against the wind and rain, never looking away from him as she simultaneously judged the distance between herself and him and the water. It was going to be a close one.

She saw the instant Asher woke up, the way his big body jerked with the shock of falling through the air.

"Asher," she shouted, and he locked gazes with her.

The ocean was growing larger and larger and larger behind him, the white crests of the swells being tossed around by the storm distinctly visible.

When Gwen got close enough, she aimed for his chest. "Shift now," she yelled.

In a silent rush, his body changed. His soul stayed in place as his physical form shifted around his essence.

Just in time for her to slam into him.

Without having to tell him, he wrapped his arms and legs around her in a way that wouldn't impede her wings, but she still caught his grunt of pain.

"Got you," his voice rumbled in her ear.

"Pretty sure I got you," she yelled back.

She wasn't built to carry her weight as well as a full-grown man who stood six-foot-four in socks and was all lean muscle and tight abs...

No thinking about tight abs when plummeting to earth, Gwen.

Wrapping her own arms and legs around him—thank the gods she'd strapped the egg to her back—Gwen held on tight and unfurled her wings, trying to catch the wind first, like a sail. The immediate jerk against their combined momentum sent a jagged shaft of pain through her back and she yelped. Asher swore but didn't let go.

Gwen fluttered her heart out, gritting her teeth against the worsening ache. Unfortunately, battling the storm and their weight, after she'd already used all her moonlight, she was rapidly losing the battle. Her breath heaved in and out of her lungs, her muscles both burning and growing heavier by the second. They were going to have to swim for a long distance in storm tossed seas controlled by whatever supernatural creature could aim lightning at planes and dragons and with the wraith possibly still out there.

Fear tried to steal the last of her breath, but she didn't have time to lose her shit.

At least I'm not alone.

That was her last thought before they hit the water, hard.

CHAPTER FOUR

Asher

Asher felt like a rock skipping across the surface before he sank under the roiling sea.

But he damn well managed to hold onto Gwen, whose head was still snapped back upon impact. She went limp in his arms like a rag doll right as a massive wave came over the top of them and then they went tumbling under water, the current pushing them deeper and deeper into darkness.

Panic rolled through him like thunder.

Shit.

Asher never fucking panicked. As a warrior, he'd dealt with worse. He cared about the people he led, of course, but they were nothing compared to Gwen. The need to protect her had always been there, but apparently, over the years of separation, it had grown roots that went bone deep. He'd do anything to get her through this.

We need air now.

But which way was up?

Holding onto Gwen with his one good arm, he kicked for what he hoped was the surface, which was a moving target thanks to the size of the swells.

Gwen jerked against his hold once, his only warning before she went wild, fighting him like a feral animal. He couldn't hold onto her, swim, and fight her at the same time, so he let go.

She spun around to face him, hands up like she was going to blast him with pixie magic, then, even in the dark water, he could see her eyes go wide.

Asher pointed up.

But she was already swimming, her strokes growing more frantic by the second. Was she out of air? The surface was so close.

With his good arm, he shoved her upward by the ass only to have her foot thrash out, right into his stomach. Uncontrollable reflex took over, and he sucked in. His lungs protested violently but coughing only sucked in more water.

Then his vision started to tunnel.

Seven hells.

While he tried to fight it, tried to swim, he was vaguely aware that Gwen had breached the surface because her head disappeared, and then her body seemed to be pulled away from him, disappearing all together. He fought. He thrashed in the water, trying to get to air, get to Gwen, but then the tunnel closed in.

Which is when a hand wrapped around his wrist and tugged. His face hit air.

Sort of.

Rain and waves pelted him, but Asher didn't give a shit as he breathed deep and hard, coughing in between gasps, trying to empty his lungs of the liquid he'd inhaled.

"Fuck me," Asher groaned when he could finally breathe.

"You okay?" A voice he'd worried he'd never hear again yelled in his ear.

Which is when he realized that Gwen still had hold of his arm.

He turned to find her dark hair floating around her in the rough seas like a damned water nymph, the pale gold of her eyes trained on his face. He'd never seen anything more beautiful.

"Are you?" he yelled back over the roar of the water.

Gwen nodded and relief speared through him.

He'd seen her plane long before he'd gotten to her, seen this blasted storm barreling down on top of her. And then the wraith…

Asher had never flown so fucking fast in all his life.

They were stuck in the middle of the ocean, the storm still raging. Who knew where the godsdamned wraith was. His arm burned like a son of bitch, not just from the lightning, but now the added ocean water. Literal salt in his wound.

But Gwen was alive, and so was he.

"I should shift—"

She shook her head. "I can hide us better at this size."

Hide? He frowned. Maybe he'd heard her wrong.

But no. She pointed up. "Whatever is controlling this storm has to be working with the wraith. They're still trying to find us."

And a giant dragon, even one just floating on the surface, was easier to see. What would they do? Duck underwater if they saw the wraith?

Gwen had always had the uncanny ability to follow his unspoken thoughts better than anyone else, and, for a breath-stealing second, he almost thought she was going to smile at him. But she turned her face away. "Trust me," she said instead.

Then she swam around him, moving her grip up his arm. He didn't know what she was going to do until suddenly she wrapped one around his chest from behind, leaving his good arm free. Shock and a very inappropriate shot of lust struck him even harder than the lightning had as she plastered herself along his back.

He'd dreamed of this. Not the storm part, but of her. Of touching her. Of her touching him.

"What are you—"

"Can you swim like this?" she asked.

Asher came back to earth with a crash. Right. She was in "save them" mode while he was drowning in sudden aching need like an asshole. "Yeah."

"Good."

Then…nothing. They just floated there like that, their legs tangling a bit as they tread seas that were battering them, equally soaked by the rain.

She'd sounded like she had a plan, but this didn't seem like a plan.

"Gwen?"

"Just waiting for the right wave."

He glanced over his shoulder to find her looking behind them. That's when a massive wave came up and over them. Asher braced, ready to grab her tighter. Only just as the wave should have hit them broadside and tossed them back under the water, she raised her hand and tiny, ember-like sparks of white swirled up and over them, flowing but not violent.

Then the wave stopped.

Dead stopped. It looked strangely like a painting suspended over the top of them, frozen mid-crest, not quite touching on the other side. And not moving. The small circle of ocean they floated in also went still.

And quiet.

The sound of both of their breathing was the only noise

in their spot, while the crash and roar of the roiling ocean was muffled outside.

"What did you do?" he asked.

She lowered her hand into the water to help them both tread but didn't let go of him. "I asked the sea for protection."

She asked... Wasn't she a moon pixie?

He'd been there the night her wings had finally appeared. Pixies didn't find out what they were until their first flight. The wings told them. She'd been so proud to be a moon pixie like her mother, her small face aglow not just with the light cast by her pure white wings, but with a radiant sort of happiness.

As if she'd read his mind again, Gwen snorted. "Pixies can talk to *all* nature. We're most in communion with our specialty, but not limited to it. You don't remember that?"

In other words, he should've known. Except every time he'd asked Goran, or Gwen, or any of their large family questions, he'd been told that only pixies were allowed to know.

But now wasn't the time to argue.

Asher kept silent.

After a second, Gwen eased up. He couldn't see her, only feel her, so he had no idea how he knew that. But he did. Maybe the grip she had on him softened.

"This is a bit like a cocoon around us, bobbing around in the ocean. It will blend in with the rest of the water from above," she finally said. "They won't be able to see us, but the crack means we can breathe."

What had she dealt with in the last decade that she'd learned that little trick?

"Smart."

"Was that sarcasm?" she grumbled.

"No."

Silence. Did she not believe him?

"Hopefully," Gwen said, "the wraith and whatever it has

controlling the weather will think we're dead and give up soon."

Asher couldn't agree more. He was injured and treading water indefinitely might be hard for him. Was she thinking of that?

"Are you okay?" she asked again.

"I'm fine," he said in a voice that the dragons under him would have taken as a sign not to ask more.

"Still a stubborn loner, I see," she murmured.

Asher's lips twitched. Gods, she sounded like she used to. Like no time had passed.

Still keeping me honest, I see. That's what he wanted to shoot back with. But the fact that she hadn't left him to die in the ocean, let alone drowned him herself, stayed his tongue. What he wanted to do was wrap his arms around her and just breathe her in, make sure she was real. But she wouldn't appreciate that.

After Goran's death, when she'd run, he'd let her. He'd known she would need time to grieve, and he'd still had a war to fight. Dragons and pixies both lived thousands of years. So, he'd given her time and space, and he'd fought for a hard-won peace.

Now the gods or the universe or whoever was in charge had dropped her right into his lap.

What did that mean?

She was probably already thinking about how she could lose him the second this was over. He didn't plan to let her. But still, trying to escape the wraith while stranded in the Flores Sea wasn't the time to try to do anything with her.

What he needed for himself was a distraction.

"Let's assume they leave," he said. "Can you fly us to land?"

A tiny growl of frustration. "No."

"Why not?" he asked without thinking. "Wings too wet?"

It was quiet enough in their magical hiding spot to hear a tiny gasp that barely reached his ears, and suddenly Asher knew instantly what she was thinking of.

The day he'd kissed her.

The one and only time he'd kissed her.

She remembered.

Inside, his dragon growled. And gods, so did he.

CHAPTER FIVE

Gwen

M emories weren't worth the pain they caused.
Gwen tried to convince herself of that. Busied herself checking on the egg, which was secure in its little pouch strapped around her.

Thankfully.

But the memories still tugged on her despite her best efforts.

That kiss had been fourteen years, two weeks, and five days ago, but it felt like yesterday. Gwen could still feel the touch of Asher's lips against hers, his hands against her cheeks.

She'd only had her wings a short time and had maybe been showing off for her brother's best friend who she'd been in love with for…well…what had felt like eons at that point. Since hitting her twenties, she'd caught him watching her, a certain light in his eyes. More and more she'd caught those looks. Looks that had sent her heart fluttering around inside her. She'd thought maybe he'd hesitated because he thought she was too young.

Pixies and dragons aged similarly, about the same as humans until they hit their twenties, and then aging slowed significantly.

But that day, the day she'd gotten her wings, she wasn't too young anymore, and she'd wanted him to know that.

In the moonlight, she'd flown out above the water of the loch near her home, wanting him to *see* her. Truly see her. But she'd overestimated her control to both fly and wield her power at the same time and ended up falling into the water.

Gods, even now her cheeks heated with mortification.

Back then a shadow overhead had her jerking her gaze upward in time to see Asher shift to human and drop into the water close by. He'd surfaced right in front of her, wiping the water and his dark hair out of his deep blue eyes with a grin that he seemed to reserve only for her.

He'd looked different back then.

She'd always thought of him as the best looking man she knew with his lean but muscular build, strong nose, thick, jet-black hair worn short, and eyes so dark blue they appeared black. Dragon shifters found mates all over the world, and for Asher, the Japanese ancestry of his great-grandmother was hinted at. He'd always claimed his unshakable courage came from that side. But when he'd kissed her that one and only time, he'd been…softer maybe? Despite the fact that he'd already been a proven warrior. Maybe the dragon wars had hardened him.

The steady strength was still the same.

"I'm here to rescue you," he'd teased.

And her heart had fluttered even harder.

Gwen had raised an eyebrow. "Do I look like I need rescuing?"

Asher had looked around them. "Can you fly?"

"No. My wings are too wet." She hadn't tucked them away in time, and they were waterlogged by then.

"But you don't need rescuing," he said, voice dropping as he swam nearer, closing the distance between them.

And the expression in his eyes, the way he looked at her, sent her heart flipflopping all over the place and a swarm of butterflies swirling through her stomach.

She couldn't look away. "No."

He'd cupped her face with his hands, their legs tangling in the water like they were now. "How about now?" he'd asked in a voice gone even lower, gruffer. Blue fire flashed in his eyes, his dragon so close to the surface. "Any rescuing needed?"

Only if dying of anticipation was a thing. "From you?" she'd whispered.

Asher had nodded slowly.

"Nah." She'd been unable to hold in her grin.

He'd moved his face closer, eyes twinkling, their breath mingling. "What about now?"

Was this really happening? she'd thought. Hells, she'd just about die of fluttery excitement. "I'm all good."

He'd moved even closer still, nudging the tip of her nose with his. "And now?" he whispered.

"Well…" she whispered back. "Maybe…"

The slow smile that reached his eyes about stopped her heart. "Gwen, if you don't want me to kiss you, say so now."

She'd gasped, and his gaze had dropped to her lips.

Gods, she'd dreamed of that kiss for years. No way would she have said anything to stop him.

The way he'd closed the distance between their lips had been the sweetest torture. Slow. Agonizingly slow, while his gaze pinned her. He'd rubbed his cheek against hers, and then even slower, tilted his head until his lips had hovered over hers.

She'd given the tiniest whimper, and that's when he'd kissed her.

And, gods, his kiss had been...everything. Soft and sweet to start, like he was making sure this was what she wanted too. But quickly, the tenor had changed. Still slow, like he was savoring every press of their lips, every sweep of his tongue against hers, and yet urgent at the same time.

And claiming.

That's what had made her glow, her happiness triggering the moonlight buried in her very skin, lighting them up along with the water around them in a heavenly light.

Asher had slowed their kisses to pull back, staring at her in something like...awe.

"I have to do something dangerous for my king," he'd said that day, gaze so intent on hers. "I won't be able to see you for a while, but when I'm done..."

"What are you doing out there?" Goran had yelled from the shore.

Gwen and Asher hadn't finished that conversation, and Asher hadn't finished the promise he'd seemed to be making. Or maybe a question. One she'd answered in her heart.

I'll wait for you.

The next day he was gone. For a year she'd thought maybe...but then Goran had died, and Asher had been part of it, in a way he'd refused to explain. In a way that looked like he either killed Goran or didn't try to save him. Neither of those things had seemed to fit. They weren't the Asher she thought she'd known. But because of his reticence, his refusal to share any information, her parents had decided that either way he was responsible, and he hadn't argued with them. He'd just done that silent thing he always did when he'd said all he was going to say.

All those hopes and dreams smashed.

So, she'd run, needing to find a new life, new dreams.

Now, the lap of the water against her skin felt the same as then. This close, even doused in salt water, she could smell the familiar scent of campfire that lingered on his skin. At least he was faced away from her. Less temptation.

You shouldn't be tempted at all, Gwendolyn Moonsoar, she chastised herself.

They'd been dealing with surviving, and just because they were now relatively safe, that didn't mean she'd forgive him for the past.

Needing the emotional distance, Gwen did her best to harden her heart. Nothing had changed. Not really. No matter how she wanted it to.

"Yeah, my wings are too wet to fly," she said in a voice gone harder and harsher.

"Gwen—"

Sunlight broke through the darkness outside, suddenly turning the wave frozen above them from a deep, murky blue to turquoise.

She blinked. "I think the wraith and its friend have gone."

"Could be a trap," he said. "Wait here."

Before she could stop him, he shrugged off her hold and swam out from under their hiding spot. Gwen moved to where the crest was suspended over the water, peeking out through the slit, but couldn't see him.

I don't like this.

Especially the way her stomach curled in worry. Worrying about him wasn't her problem anymore. Except…

"All clear, I think," Asher called from somewhere off to the right.

By the time she swam out from under the wave, then released it, Asher had shifted. A massive, dark blue dragon floated in the water beside her like a duck.

Right. Dragons had hollow bones.

"What are you doing?" she demanded. "What if—"

"Wraiths can't be in sunlight." His voice ping-ponged around in her head.

"But the thing that's controlling the storm could," she pointed out. "Aren't you supposed to be some bad ass dragon general or something now? Seems pretty obvious—"

He jerked his chin off to the southeast. Sure enough, massive, dark storm clouds were visible in the distance, but far enough away that they were safe for the moment.

Now she looked like the asshole.

Regroup, she told herself. *Focus on a plan. What next?*

"We should swim the opposite direction," Asher said, beating her to it. *"Find an island, preferably inhabited, and then figure out our next steps."*

Despite her determination not to care, Gwen frowned, checking out his right wing, which was folded back. "You can't fly?"

"No." Without warning, Asher scooped her out of the water with his left wing.

"Whoa!" Gwen squeaked as she wobbled on her hands and knees. "A little heads-up next time, yeah?" Then she crawled across the thinner membrane to his back. He had his spikes laid down, allowing her to sit with her knees drawn up.

"Ready?" he asked.

She rolled her eyes at the back of his head, wicked spikes, and all. Did he think she was scared or something? She'd changed a lot since he last saw her. "Ready."

Using his tail and back legs to propel them, Asher took off through the waters. All Gwen could do was sit and let him get them somewhere safer. But there were things she could do. First, she moved the egg pouch around so that it was strapped around her waist and basically cradled between her legs and body. Then, she unfurled her wings, letting them dry in the breeze generated by their momentum.

But that was it. Otherwise, she was just waiting to get to their destination.

After a little while, with nothing to look at but dragon, water, and an island in the distance, but mostly dragon, Gwen reached out and poked a finger at one of his scales. She'd always found Asher's scales fascinating—supple, more like a lizard's underbelly, but hard at the same time, and reflective, like liquid sapphires lay trapped inside each one.

Absentmindedly, she traced a pattern over it, feeling the smoothness like a balm, reminding her of the rose quartz worry stone her mother had given her to keep close while she was so far from home.

Suddenly, the scales under her hand and all around her undulated, like a bird ruffling its feathers, and Asher made a sound between a grunt and a groan. *"Tickles,"* he rumbled inside her head.

Gwen jerked her hand away. Heat flamed up her face, because he was being kind, helping save her the embarrassment. She knew damn well that what he felt through his scales wasn't ticklish. He'd once told her that it felt... tempting.

What had she been thinking? She put her hands to her flaming cheeks, glad he couldn't see her right now.

Wait a minute. Between the two of us, I should not be the one on the wrong foot.

Wrapping thirteen years of resentment around her like a shield, Gwen straightened.

"Why are you here?" she asked.

Asher hesitated. Only a smidge, but she caught it. *"Delilah got in touch to say that she'd lost her courier. I volunteered as a tracker before I knew it was you."*

It was really stupid that her heart sank at his choice of

words, which only added to her growing irritation. "How very gallant of you," she said in a flat voice.

"You know I didn't mean it that way."

"I don't actually," she said in a voice heavy with finality. "After all, we're strangers now, aren't we?"

Not a statement of regret or wishing. Simply what was.

Asher said nothing, but this time, for some odd reason his usual silence felt like…hurt.

Which couldn't be right. After all, she'd only stated a truth. A truth that had been going on for a while. So why did it feel like a rock had settled in her stomach?

Maybe it would be better to avoid any topics involving the two of them. Focus on getting the egg to its destination safely.

Gwen cleared her throat. "What do you think was driving that storm?"

After a second, he answered. *"A thunderbird maybe, but it would be far from home."*

She cocked her head, thinking. "Maybe a demigod?"

His grunt was basically a "could be."

"Or worse," she muttered, propping her chin on her knees. The power and control of that storm had been… specific.

The island was growing larger and larger on the horizon. At the speed they were going, it wouldn't take much longer to get there.

Gwen sighed. At least then, she could get some physical distance between them. Maybe facing Asher in a space where they weren't quite so reliant on each other would stop the memories. Stop her from wanting things that couldn't be. This felt so much like the dreams that haunted her almost every night. The ones where Goran had never died, and Asher had returned to her from his mission as a spy in Thanatos's court. The ones where she and Asher were actually mates. The ones where he touched her and she touched him, and they...

Stop it, Gwen.

She must've made a noise or something because Asher turned his head just slightly. "All right?" he asked.

"Fine."

Or she would be once she got away from him, and the confusing, muddled mess his nearness was turning her into.

Asher was involved in Goran's death. She should hate him. She should want nothing to do with him. She should focus on her damn job.

Get to that island. Heal up enough to get off it. Then get her delivery made and get the hells away from him. End of story.

So why did that plan feel so...wrong?

CHAPTER SIX

Asher

The storms still hung in the distance, flashes of lightning penetrating the blue skies several miles out. At least they weren't close.

Yet.

Asher dragged himself up the beach, then waited to shift until Gwen climbed down. Somewhere along the way she'd gone quiet on him, like she'd remembered that she hated him. So she said nothing now.

Neither did he.

What could he say anyway? The important stuff would only kick in that godsdamned blood oath and get him killed.

So he shifted, then sat in the sand, uninjured elbow propped on his drawn-up knees, giving himself a second to recover. His muscles were rubber after flying so far, the fight, and then the long swim to land.

But still, what the hells?

He'd never needed to stop and rest before, except after what Goran did to him in his last moment. That was the only time. Dragons had stamina. They were physical creatures. And they healed fast. So what was going on now?

Trying to be subtle about it, he checked his arm.

The entire scorch mark was visible because the lightning had fried off the sleeve of his shirt. But at least the hole in his flesh wasn't gaping and oozing anymore. Not that it looked great. From the angry red gash in his elbow, spreading in either direction, his skin was charred black. With the way dragons healed, it should have improved more than this by now, even while he was swimming.

Hells.

He glanced at Gwen, who had her back to him, egg strapped to her back now. Her hands were on her hips as she walked down the beach a little, seemingly checking out the island they'd landed on. They'd circled from the water and seen zero signs of life, but getting to an inhabited island would have to wait until he'd rested more.

Gods, she looked amazing. Her long hair had dried in a tangle down her back, and her black leggings and t-shirt were salt crusted. Not a lick of makeup. And she was… gorgeous.

Obviously, she was working out what they needed to do next, unlike him. He was just sitting here lusting and wishing and…

Focus the fuck up, Ash.

He turned his gaze out to sea, because clearly any view with Gwen in it was a distraction. Right. First things first.

"We should—"

Gwen spun around, cutting him off. "I think the wind while you swam might've dried my wings enough," she said. Her hand went to the strap of her pack, unclasping it and dropping the egg to the ground. "If I can fly, I can get us help."

Her wings unfurled from her back, and his body surged to aching life at the sight. Asher scowled at himself. Damn it all, she could have given him more warning than that. He'd always been fascinated by her wings, turned on by the full sight of her. Did she not realize that?

His dick hardened, pressing against his jeans zipper, his dragon also surging. The urge to step closer for a better look, to see if her wings had changed at all through the years, to *touch* her, had him clenching his jaw.

Because he'd *never* do that without permission.

Taking a long, slow, silent breath, he wrangled and tied up his reactions and his dragon tight as he tried to take a more scientific view.

Pixie wings were a miraculous creation.

She didn't need to leave her back bare to unfurl them. Whatever magic pixies possessed worked so that their wings appeared to just sort of come out of their clothes, and when they disappeared, no one could tell the difference between a pixie and a human. Formed like butterfly wings with four distinct sections, two on each side, that overlaid each other but could work both in tandem and independently, no two pixie's wings were alike. The colors and patterns were distinct and individual like a fingerprint.

Gwen slowly maneuvered like she was stretching them, feeling them out, but not fluttering yet.

Her wings were somehow both white and translucent at the same time, iridescent with hints of all the colors of the rainbow as they moved, even brighter in sunlight. They were also larger than many others because of her lineage, forming horns at the tops, spreading out wide behind her and then dropping into swallowtail-like loops at the bottom that brushed the ground when she walked. Scattered throughout were dots that were ringed in gleaming gold. And in moonlight, when her wings were out, Gwen disappeared in the shafts of soft white light entirely, like a mirage. An illusion.

Like Gwen herself. At least as far as he was concerned.

So real, and yet if he reached for her, she'd dissolve, leaving him alone again.

Asher watched as Gwen fluttered her wings so that it looked like a rainbow of colors hovered behind her in a cloud with flashes of gold catching the sunlight. She lifted off, flying slowly higher as she tested herself, making it about twenty feet up. Then a pained gasp tore from her and she dropped, arms pinwheeling.

Asher lunged to his feet, and just barely made it under her in time to catch her, but thanks to his injured arm, pain bolted through him, and he crumpled under the impact, tumbling them both to the ground. He tried to roll them so that he took the brunt of the fall, but, thanks to landing on a bit of a hill, they rolled again and ended up with Gwen pinned under him.

They stared at each other, sharing a breath for stomach-clenching moment. "Gwen," he whispered.

She blinked, then gasped, and then shoved at his shoulders.

Asher squeezed his eyes shut, trying to breathe through the throbbing slashing through him.

Gwen shoved again. "Get off me."

The urgency in her voice cut through the pain and he opened his eyes to find hers wide with...anger? Fear maybe?

Did she think he'd hurt her the way he'd hurt Goran?

Fuck.

She shoved again, sending another shard of agony lancing down his arm. With a grunt, he grabbed both her wrists in his one good hand and pulled them above her head, pinning her in the sand. "Let's get one thing straight, Gwen. I would never hurt you. Not if I could help it, but you're hurting me right now."

She went dead still beneath him. Her breasts pressed into him with every ragged breath she took as she stared back at him with wide, apologetic eyes.

His dragon pressed to get to her. To be released to curl protectively around her. He'd liked having her touching when they'd been in the sea, but this was more immediate, more urgent. Almost like his animal side didn't trust him to keep her safe.

Asher pressed his lips together, casting his gaze over the delicate lines of her face. He clamped down on the urge to run a finger over the silken skin of her cheek. She'd hate that.

"Are you going to calm down now, so I can let you up?" he asked instead.

Wide eyes narrowed to a glare. "You're touching my wing," she said in a strained voice.

"Fuck," he muttered as he scrambled off her as fast as he could without making it worse.

Gwen surged to her feet the second she was free, facing him with cheeks turning rosier by the second and shifting her weight from foot to foot.

Touching a pixie's wings was extremely personal, and, for the pixie, pleasurable. If you did it right, it could even be orgasm inducing.

Was she fighting that sensation right now?

Did his touch make her...

His cock, already aroused by the sight of her wings and then having her under him that way, went hard as fucking dragon steel.

Quit that shit, Asher snarled at himself in his head. *You should not be turned on by an involuntary response she can't control.*

But he couldn't look away.

He stared at her, and she stared at him, though her gaze kept skittering away before returning.

Stop being an asshole. She wants nothing to do with you.

Her brows lowered as she glanced off to the right, only to glance back again, like she couldn't decide what she wanted to do with him.

A thousand layers of blame and guilt surfaced, and he forced his gaze away, hands curling into fists at his sides. Once upon a time, watching all her emotions cross her features this way would have made him laugh or made him want to kiss her. She couldn't hide her feelings to save her life.

Now, it only twisted the knife-like feeling in his chest even further.

They needed a moment. Maybe more than a moment.

Eating was a priority. So was finding water. Definitely finding a place to hide in case the storm came back, or, when night fell, the wraith returned. He glanced in the direction of the clouds in the distance. Whatever was after the egg was a determined motherfucker.

"I'm going to get us fish," he tossed over his shoulder, his voice coming out a growl that was decidedly grumpy sounding. He didn't mean it that way. No use explaining though. "Stay where I can see you." Now he was issuing orders.

Maybe asshole had become his default setting, but no way in the seven hells was he letting Gwen was out of his sight.

Not when the storm could barrel down on them at any second. Not when the wraith was still out there searching. Not when the mere sight of her still filled him with need.

CHAPTER SEVEN

Asher

Asher stalked off, wading back into the water and ignoring the renewed sting of salt water in his wound as he shifted.

Scooping up fish with his one good wing turned out to be easy, and he returned to the beach within twenty minutes or so. Using a single shifted talon, he gutted his catches, then started gathering wood for a fire—the one thing dragons were never without.

Acutely aware that Gwen was foraging around in the brush nearby, he tried to focus on his task as he stacked wood up on the spit of sand, and, using his own spark, ignited it. Quickly, he got the fish cooking on long, shiny leaves laid out on a flat rock close to but not right in the flames. He squatted by the fish, turning the leaves like hands of a clock to cook the other sides better.

Suddenly, a shadow fell over what he was doing. Gwen standing close.

He swore. Damn pixies never seemed to move, and yet somehow would suddenly be right where they wanted to be. Sneaking up on a dragon was both unusual, and sexy as hell.

"Don't sneak up on me," he grumbled.

After a beat, she set several mangos in the sand at his feet. "Here."

She'd used to talk to him with warmth and affection in her voice, and at one point…more. Sweetly more. Innocently more. He'd waited a long time for her to grow up, catch up to him. And then she had, but the timing had been all wrong. All they'd had was that one kiss before he'd gone off to be a spy and fight a war.

Clenching his teeth together, Asher looked away, then grunted with annoyance. He'd burned the damn fish. He grabbed the rock they were cooking on and yanked it away from the heat.

"Did you burn yourself?" Gwen asked, reaching for his hand.

He pulled away and could feel her gaze on him as her hand hovered in the air between them. Touching her more was a bad fucking idea right now.

"Dragon," he pointed out with a shrug. Heat resistant, even as a human.

She huffed. "Right."

"Sit," he said. "Eat."

They'd both feel better, and then they could come up with a plan.

He could see by the stubborn tensing around her eyes that Gwen didn't want to agree with anything he had to say, or maybe the way he'd said it. Or ordered it more like.

Asher swallowed a sigh of frustration with himself—the years of fighting had turned him into someone harder, he'd known that, but it hadn't been so obvious as it was with her. Deliberately he sat and turned his attention to carving up the mango she'd brought in a way that they could just pluck pieces of the sweet center out. Anything to keep from meeting her gaze. A few minutes later, she walked abruptly away, and every muscle in him tensed, then he blew out a small breath when she came back and set the egg down close to the fire before she held out her hands for a leaf of fish.

For the first time since he'd tackled that wraith midair, they had calm. One that might not last, but still…she was safe, for now.

And she was with him.

Gods, he'd missed her face. Her voice. The scent that followed her, fresh and clean and sort of misty at the same time. Like dew. Like moonlight.

She was within touching, and it took everything he had not to close his eyes and inhale. Not to grab her wrist and tug her into his lap.

Instead, he handed the fish to her, careful not to touch her when he did. Then she made her way around the fire to sit as far from him as she could get. Stuffing the sting of disappointment down deep, he grabbed his own meal, shoving the much-needed protein in his mouth. Food would help with the healing.

As if she'd followed his train of thought, Gwen eyed his left arm, brows scrunching up in adorable concern. She said nothing, silently chewing, until finally, "I used all my moonlight on the wraith," she said a few minutes later. "If I can absorb more tonight, then I'll feel much better."

"*All* your moonlight?"

She flashed him an annoyed look. "What's that supposed to mean?"

Asher paused with a chunk of fish meat halfway to his mouth. "Exactly what it means."

Gwen sat up so straight, a steel beam might as well have been welded to her spine. "So you're judging me now? For doing what was necessary to save us both?"

"No judgment." He attempted to say this calmly.

Her expression begged to differ. "Oh, there was judgment."

Asher blew out a sharp breath. So did his dragon. Clearly, she wanted to pick a fight. Maybe she'd decided that loaded silence wasn't enough of a clue and to shove her anger at him now. Maybe she just needed the distance. Either way, he had no right to fight back. Her brother *was* dead because of him. She deserved to hate him.

"Your father always said the first rule of being a pixie was never to use all your power at once." He tried to sound reasonable.

Apparently, he'd failed because that only earned him another glare. "I don't need you to give me lectures on my own abilities. I know what I'm doing."

Asher tried to keep his own frown tucked away, but it took effort. There was pissed at him, and then there was unreasonable. "Did I say otherwise?"

Hells, he'd been damn impressed so far.

"But you *are* questioning my ability to know when to use my power or not."

"I'm not —"

"I've been doing fine without you around," she snapped. "I'm a-fucking-mazing at my job, and definitely not a little girl anymore."

That was for damn sure.

Gwen blew out a huffy breath. "You haven't changed a bit. Coming here, all heroic, to save poor little Gwen, right? Throwing my father in my face."

Screw not being allowed to be irritated. "Not even close to right," he didn't bother to keep the growl out of his voice this time. "Delilah sent me." He shoved more fish in his mouth and angry-chewed.

Surprisingly, Gwen didn't say anything in return. Not that he looked at her. He couldn't. Seeing the heat of blame in her eyes when she used to look at him with something closer to adoration was like being slowly gutted with a dull paring knife.

"Let's just focus on getting out of here," Gwen finally said.

Asher shot her a discerning look, taking in the way she hunched over her food, the way she turned slightly away from him, the way she wouldn't meet his gaze, focused on her now picked apart fish bones and the mangled mango.

"Fine by me," he said.

With a huff, Gwen got to her feet and wandered down to the water to wash off her hands. "We need a plan in case the wraith comes for us before we manage to get off this rock."

Something in her voice, the way she held herself, the solid confidence of knowledge and experience reflected in her pale eyes caught him.

Gwen *was* different.

Well, of course she was. Time changed everyone.

But before…she'd been softer, sweeter, more…innocent. He didn't see much of that in her anymore. Instead, it was replaced by a hardness around her eyes. Same as him.

Was she lonely, too?

Even surrounded by his people, with position and purpose to center him, not to mention friends, if he let himself call them that, Asher damn sure was.

She shot him a questioning frown when he didn't answer right away, and Asher deliberately schooled his expression. He didn't want her to catch sight of the longing in him. He wouldn't hurt her more if he could help it.

When her frown deepened, he rushed to redirect. "I had a

satellite phone with me, but I must have lost it when we took that dip in the ocean."

Gwen tugged at a gold chain around her neck, pulling out a charm that was a thick golden disk. "This is a tracer. I turned it off when I realized I was being followed by something in Australia. That was to get Delilah's attention, also in case it's how I was found, but I can turn it back on. She'll send more help."

Asher shook his head. "She found your flight plan. They'll have an idea of where we went down. When I don't check in, Ladon and Meilin will send more after us." Although that would take several days from either the green dragon mountain or from the Australian colony. "Let's give them a day or so to get closer. If we can't get ourselves off the island by then, then we'll turn your tracer on."

At least she didn't scowl or try to argue this time, simply slipping the necklace back under her shirt with a nod. "In that case, our next priorities are water and shelter."

Asher nodded.

She looked around them. "We should split up."

"No." The word came out as more of a harsh growl than he intended.

Now came the scowl as she whipped her gaze back to him. "It'll be faster."

"It'll be more dangerous." If he'd used that tone on one of the dragons under his command, they would have stopped talking immediately.

Gwen rolled her eyes. "The storm is in the distance, and we have a little daylight left." She glanced to the west where the sun was starting to drop, but not yet lengthening the shadows.

"I go where you go."

That earned him another eye roll. "Then I guess we'll try to do both at the same time."

"Fine." He got to his feet and dug under the fire.

"What are you doing?" she asked.

"We can bury the egg here. My fire will keep it warm while we look." And not even a wraith would dare to touch dragon fire.

Surprisingly, she didn't argue with that one. Gwen glanced up at the trees and Asher followed her gaze. Coconuts.

"I don't think there's enough of them to be our main source of water," she said.

He grunted an agreement. Coconuts didn't produce a lot of water, and, at least as far as he could see, there was only this small clump of the trees here.

"But," she said. "We could use them to carry water if we find it."

Smart Gwen. But something about how fast she'd found that solution sat wrong.

When had she had to learn survival skills? Had she been in situations like this before? Had she been in danger?

He'd been oblivious.

When he'd allowed himself to think of her, he'd pictured her safely ensconced with a different flutter of pixies. Maybe teaching the young to use their powers. She'd always been gifted that way.

Instead, she'd been Delilah's courier.

Of course she'd been in fucking danger before.

Danger he hadn't been there to protect her from.

I really am an asshole.

Once they'd pulled a few coconuts down and he'd hollowed them out, she walked off the beach without even a smidge of hesitation, and for a second Asher let himself watch after her.

Even after the fight and the swimming, she moved with a subtle, delicate grace that was partly her pixie nature, but even more…just Gwen. She flowed the way moonlight did, slipping and spilling between the cracks.

Gods, he'd missed her.

He'd spent the last thirteen years stuffing that ache down deep, focusing on the need in front of him—the war of kings. But now that she was here…

Could he let her go again?

Did he even have a choice?

The last thing he'd ever want to do was make anything worse for her. Which meant keeping his hands off, and his thoughts to himself.

This was going to be a long couple of days.

Suddenly, a roll of thunder reached him from the distance and they both turned to look. Sure enough the storm had come closer. Still not close enough to affect them, but there was no doubt they were being hunted. Godsdamn it.

They'd better move fast.

CHAPTER EIGHT

Gwen

"I told you it would get dark faster than you thought," Asher growled back at Gwen as he ran ahead of her, only pausing to hold branches so they didn't whack her as they went past.

"We need water," she pointed out.

Not that they'd found it. All they'd had was coconut water so far.

But thanks to her insisting, they'd strayed too far out searching. By the time they'd gotten to the beach to retrieve the egg from where it had been safely buried while they searched, darkness was crawling its way across the skies, which were now purple on the horizon. They needed to get to the tiny cavern they'd found and hole up for the night. Quick.

Zigzagging around trees and bushes, Gwen followed Asher to an outcropping of rocks, skirting them inland, having to navigate around more trees and vegetation, until the roll of the waves could no longer be heard.

She only started to breathe easier when the long crevice that was the opening to their hiding spot came into view. There was only one small entrance, and no other way to get at them in there. Asher's dragon fire would keep them safe if they were found.

They were maybe a few yards from the entrance when a movement in the trees ahead to their right caught her attention. Gwen didn't have to look twice.

Unfurling her wings, she sped up and grabbed Asher by the shirt, yanking him to the side so that he stepped directly into a wide shaft of moonlight. In the same instant, she wrapped her wings and one arm around him, clamping her other hand over his mouth to smother any surprised noise he might make.

"Stay quiet," she whispered as she moved them quickly through the beam of moonlight, so they weren't in the same spot she'd used to make them disappear.

Only when they stopped did she slowly lower her arm. Just as a hand of swirling shadow reached through the shaft of moonlight where she'd hidden them.

A wraith in the darkness.

Damn. She'd thought she'd gotten them far enough away.

For a split second, a memory surfaced. One of her laughing as she used moonlight to hide from the very dragon shifter in her arms right now. Only this wasn't a human hand after her.

And this definitely wasn't a game.

The storm was closer, but not on top of them yet. Was this the same wraith they'd been dealing with all along? If it was, the bastard was hard to kill. Or was there more than one, and this was a scout that got lucky?

The hand reached again.

Icy fear froze its way down her spine, and she clenched her fists against it.

Gwen and Asher stayed still and silent, and she prayed the wraith wouldn't look down. She could hide them in the white light streaming between vegetation, but the indent of their feet in the sand would be visible.

She stared at the shadowy hand clawing around for them, heart tripping so loud she worried the wraith might hear.

"I know you're here, pixie." The sweet sigh of the wraith's whisper—a sound even sirens envied, meant to lure prey closer—was at direct odds with the threat in the words. "Come out now, and I'll be nice and let your dragon shifter live."

Asher twitched against her but made no other reaction.

It was getting closer, forcing Gwen to lean them further back without moving their feet. Even if the wraith could penetrate the moonlight with its hand, it couldn't see inside it. The light would blind it. Unfortunately, given where it had cornered them, with shafts of moonlight broken by shadows, escaping would be…difficult.

But maybe she could distract it. Give Asher a chance to hide with the egg, which he was carrying, while she got to unbroken moonlight where she could safely hide indefinitely.

She glanced around them, taking in the options and escape routes available. Not many. There had to be a way out of here that didn't involve a throwdown with the wraith. She couldn't fight a wraith. Even with its weakness to her light, it was more powerful and more dangerous than she'd ever be. Dragon fire would obliterate it, but it would also gain the attention of whatever drove the storms. And possibly more wraiths if they were dealing with multiple.

So she had one shot—blind it and she and Asher could split up and hide.

Gwen held her breath as those wispy fingers of darkness continued to dig around inside the shaft of moonlight where they hid, keeping an eye on both it and the edge of the beam. Asher's shoulders would be visible if they leaned any further. Soon they'd have no choice but to move their feet, which would make their location much more obvious.

Stomach clenching around her fear, Gwen held her breath and slowly started absorbing the moonbeam, drawing it inside her through her skin.

She couldn't fly up, but she could use her wings to propel her faster along the ground. If she could just reach the beach…

The hand moved the other way, and she almost breathed an audible sigh of relief, but stopped herself. Even the slightest noise and it would know exactly where they were. Seizing the moment of reprieve, she pulled even more light into her body, the sensation not warm but cool, like the moon herself. At the same time, she looked at Asher and, using military hand signals, told him where they should both go.

He eyed her, not shaking his head, but not happy.

She eyed him right back.

"Trust me," she mouthed the words.

He gave the slightest shake of his head and the shaft around them eddied—just barely—but with a triumphant hiss the wraith reached straight for her.

A luminous surge of moonlight-powered energy burst from her very soul as Gwen shot forward. The wraith's howl of pain chased her as she flitted through the trees, abandoning Asher to his own hiding. She raced from shaft to shaft of moonlight, passing through a few patches of darkness as she avoided branches.

Don't stop. Don't look. Keep going.

She gritted her teeth against the dull ache—trying to slow

Asher's fall when they'd plummeted into the ocean had pulled a muscle or something—her wings beat as fast as they could, using the light she'd absorbed to boost her speed. Any second darkness could catch her or pluck her wings from her back. Her skin crawled with the anticipation of it. Only experience kept her from looking over her shoulder.

Finally, she burst onto the long stretch of sand with a gasp of relief.

Though she wasn't out of danger yet. Gwen went dead still.

The wraith can't follow me out here.

Not when a full moon glowed with angelic innocence in the star-bitten skies.

With no warning, a lasso of darkness grabbed her by the foot and yanked her off her feet. What the fuck? She'd never seen a wraith do anything like that with light. Gwen didn't have a chance to fight it before she was being dragged back into the trees, the darkness closing in on her fast.

Then an explosion of blue flame lit up the night.

A single burst in a long stream. The wraith's scream cut off almost as abruptly as it started and when the fire stopped, the creature was gone. A tiny pile of ash lay on the ground, blending into the sand.

Asher stood nearby and she shot him a wide-eyed look. He'd done that without shifting. Only the most powerful dragons could do that. When had he learned?

"Do you think the storm creature saw?" she asked in a whisper.

Before Asher could answer, a plop of wetness hit her face.

Rain.

Seven hells.

CHAPTER NINE

GWEN

"Run." Asher took off across the beach, obviously expecting her to follow.

Which she did.

Gwen was tempted to pull out her wings again to fly faster than she could run but knew she might need them more later. So instead, she awkwardly ran through the deep sand in his wake, pelted by fat raindrops that were so unnaturally cold it felt like being hit with snow, each strike stinging against her skin.

Her clothes and hair were plastered to her by the time they ducked into the too-small crevice they'd found earlier, but at least it protected them from the weather.

"I swear the storm was far away when I used my fire," Asher said in a voice she'd only ever heard from him once before. Asher was always serious, but this was deadly grim, and heavy. With guilt if she was reading him right.

The same way he'd sounded when he'd come with news of Goran's death.

His gaze was focused over her head, on the narrow entrance to their hiding spot. "Hopefully they weren't able to see exactly which island the fire was on." He paused, and his gaze lowered to her face slowly. Achingly slow. A glitter in his eyes she hadn't seen since…

"I won't let them hurt you," he said. A growl rose up from deep inside him, a rolling bass that was far from human, so animalistic, so feral that the fine hairs all over her stood straight up.

His dragon.

He sounded…

She swallowed.

Asher sounded like she was his to protect.

Only I'm not his to protect. I'm not his anything.

Okay, so she was disregarding the fact that he'd been sent here by her boss, his king, and the green dragon queen to help her. That *did* kind of make her his to protect, which sat with her about as comfortably as sand up her ass crack. But this kind of growl…

This was different.

Even as she wanted to lean into the spark of warmth that settled in the center of her chest.

Damn it.

Mission or no, he didn't need to sound like…like he'd tear anything that came near her limb from limb and enjoy it.

Like she was his mate.

He didn't need to make this harder on her. More confusing because of feelings she'd thought she'd managed to bury years ago.

But hadn't.

And those dreams she'd thought she'd buried with her feelings were still there too. Against her will, her treacherous heart fluttered, just because of the way he was *watching* her.

The deep blue of his eyes should have appeared black inside their small cavern, but his fire had ignited in those depths. The flickering glow cast a blue light over his features, taut with…

Her breath lodged in her throat.

She forced herself to do the opposite of what her confuddled heart was telling her to do and took a step back. It didn't help. A second step back, and she was in the rain again. Asher's hand caught her in a flash, tugging her back under the cover of shelter, as he also shuffled further inside, taking her with him. Even though he dropped his hold immediately, she still felt his touch like a brand.

The gods or fates or whoever had landed them in this predicament had to be howling with laughter right about now.

Meanwhile, Gwen was starting to regret the fact that the only orgasms she'd had in a very long time were by her own hand. Not that the previous ones with other partners had been all that great. She'd tried to find love. It hadn't worked for her. But now…now the warmth in her chest was morphing to a different kind of burn, an ache settling deeper inside her that wanted…more.

From one look. From one touch.

What am I thinking?

Familiarity. That's all this reaction was. Familiarity and forced proximity.

Not the most convincing argument, but she latched onto it all the same.

She pulled her shoulders back. "We might as well get settled."

The fire in Asher's eyes banked, his expression going flat like he'd shut down every emotion. "Not a lot of room in here." He glanced around them, maybe able to see more than she could. "But it'll do for the night," he tacked on.

Hopefully.

He reached toward her face, and Gwen jerked back this time.

Asher tensed. Almost imperceptibly, but enough she caught it.

He cleared his throat "I was just going to…" He reached out again and pulled a leaf from her hair, showing it to her before he dropped it. Then he unstrapped the egg and moved the rest of the way into the tiny space, burying it in the sand in a natural crook of the rock.

Gwen turned her back on him and pretended to be busy wringing out her clothes and trying not to think about flaming eyes, ridged muscles, that low growl, or how it felt to be the one protected, and not the one doing the protecting, for the first time in a very long time.

He's the reason Goran is dead. Either get answers or get this over with and get away from him again.

She dropped her chin to her chest, eyes closed, trying to make herself agree with that sound logic. Could she walk away from him a second time? She'd thought she'd grown stronger than that.

"We need to get you warm." His voice came from behind her.

Gwen frowned, first at the words, and then even harder at the realization that she was shivering.

"That rain was *not* tropical," Asher pointed out next.

As if proving his point, wind whipped into their hiding spot, carrying with it a frozen bite of winter and she shivered even harder. "I'll be fine."

The hole of silence at her back seemed to grow and grow.

"You can hate me all you want, Gwen," he finally said in a

hard voice that gave away no emotions. "But don't let it drive you to poor choices."

Gwen stiffened so hard she was surprised her back didn't spasm. "I don't…hate you," she said in a soft voice.

More silence. She refused to turn around and try to see the emotions in his eyes. So stoic, his face was almost always a blank, but his eyes, that's what gave him away.

But she didn't want to see if he was hurt, or guilty, or didn't care, or whatever it was he felt about all of this.

"You don't?"

She gave her head a small shake, glaring at the sand at her feet. "I can't forgive you, Asher. But I could never hate you."

Her young heart had loved him too much for that.

"I…see." Another long stretch of silence.

Finally she turned around to find his hair standing on end like he'd been running his fingers through it. "What do you suggest?"

His frown was a question all by itself.

"About the cold," she clarified.

His wince told her she wasn't going to love his answer. "We can't risk dragon fire."

She nodded. The storm was too close.

"But even in human form I can keep us both warm."

Human form. Her eyes widened.

He meant snuggling up with each other for body heat, or in his case, animal heat. An entire night plastered to his side. Given the way her feelings about him were all over the damn place, that sounded like torture. But he wouldn't have suggested that if there was any other option.

She blew out a frustrated breath and blinked as it misted on the air. The drop in temperature was that sharp.

"I'll take first watch," she said.

Asher hummed in what she assumed was an agreement, then sat down on the sandy floor—at least it wasn't rocky—

with his back against one of the small cavern's walls. He winced, but didn't complain, instead waving her over. Taking a silent breath, she tried to calm her nerves, to get her heart to stop tripping over itself as she carefully sat beside Asher in the sand.

"This will keep you warmer," he said in a voice that sounded both reluctant and apologetic.

"What will—"

Asher scooped her up and deposited her between his legs, her back to his chest. A low sound from her memories, like the bellows of a forge, came from behind and around her... and then lovely warmth seeped into every part of her.

"I'm going to put my arms around your middle," he said, lips close to her ear.

It took every ounce of her self-control not to shiver for a completely different, very inconvenient reason. "Okay," she murmured.

He slid his arms up under hers and across her stomach, his palm flattening against her belly. More warmth seeped into her. With her knees drawn up, all he had to do was move his fingers a tiny bit downward and...

Get your mind off anything that has to do with his fingers and your body, Gwendolyn Moonsoar.

Except now that her imagination had gone there, memory after memory of dreams she'd had of the two of them together over the years barraged her without mercy. A holdover from the days when she'd craved his touch, when she'd thought they had a future. That's all this was.

Although, come to think of it, a certain part of his anatomy was pressed to her lower back right now.

A hard part of him.

Oh my gods.

She tried not to wriggle. Tried not to feel it. Tried like hells not to react to it.

"You should sleep," she said. Maybe if he did, she could breathe easier.

The hand at her belly tensed a little, then relaxed. "Wake me in a few hours," was all he said in return.

He seemed to adjust his position somewhat, and then went still and silent. It still took a while, but eventually his breathing turned deeper and heavier, and she knew he was out. Asher had always been able to sleep anywhere at any time.

Military training, he'd used to say.

Not Gwen.

Especially not like this.

CHAPTER TEN

Gwen

Warmth surrounded Gwen, and the hand softly stroking her belly drew a contented smile to her lips. Humming low in her throat, she leaned into the solid body pressed up against her back. She didn't remember falling asleep.

The dream again.

The one that had caught her up in its fantasy more nights than it hadn't over the last thirteen years. The one where Asher had mated her, built a life with her, and would make love to her every day. In her dreams was the only place she could allow herself not to be mad at him. In her dreams, she could touch and be touched and just enjoy. No guilt. Her dreams weren't real—just in her head. The only problem was the guilt that came with waking, for still wanting him. Okay, there were two problems. The fact that she was guaranteed to wake up disappointed in the end also sucked.

Maybe this time he wouldn't disappear when things started getting good. Those teasing fingers continued to play over her belly, but she wanted them lower, so she scooted a bit trying to hint, and a low chuckle sent an answering shiver of need prickling over her skin. Impatience had her taking his hand and showing him exactly where she wanted his touch.

"Here?" Laughter hung in Asher's sleep laden voice as he trailed those questing fingers under the band of her leggings and past the barrier of her panties but stopped short of the right spot.

"Lower," she whispered.

"Mmmm… Here?" His fingers explored.

She hummed, arching to chase what she wanted.

Don't wake up yet, she urged the dream. *Not yet. Not—*

Finally, he swept a finger lightly over the bundle of nerves at the junction of her thighs, and Gwen pressed back into him with a sigh of bliss as sensation lit through her, joining the warmth of their bodies. Maybe she'd actually get to reach the end of this dream for once. Usually she woke up unfulfilled and frustrated as hells, and angry at herself for indulging yet again.

But for now…

Hanging onto the dream as tightly as she could, she sighed and moaned and melted into the touches that were making her hotter and wetter and…oh gods. Did she dare ask for more?

If she did, maybe it would dissolve the fantasy.

"I need to be inside you, love," Asher whispered in a need-laden groan.

"Gods, yes."

She fumbled, inching down her leggings and panties together, baring herself to him as he freed himself from his jeans. Faster was better. If they were fast enough, maybe they could get this done before her mind cottoned on and yanked her out of it.

The dream kept going.

He lifted her leg, nudging at her entrance, and then nuzzled her neck. "You're sure?"

"I'm sure."

"Thank gods." Then he murmured something she didn't quite catch. Something like, "Please don't disappear on me this time. Not yet."

Or maybe her own wishing was filtering to him. To dream Asher.

Then he pressed forward, the thick, pulsing length of him sliding deep with ease—gods she was so turned on for him, slick with desire. When he was fully seated inside her, Asher paused, and his entire body shuddered around her, his cock swelling, stretching her. "Yes," he whispered into her neck. "Like that."

She breathed through the pulsing now taking up a beat inside her, in time with his body.

"Stay with me," he whispered.

"I'm with you."

Finally. Tears seeped out at the ache of every unfulfilled dream she'd been yanked out of over the years. Those dreams had carried not only the frustration of not reaching completion, but the slap in the face of what she'd lost all over again. Along with a wallop of guilt for missing him at all when she should have been angry with him.

Not this time though. This time, they'd get there.

Her sighs turned into a hitch as he found her clit with his fingers, then in a slow, decadent dance he moved and he touched, timing each brush of those tantalizing fingers with each surge inside her.

Her dream couldn't be so cruel as to rip this away from her now. Could it?

It didn't take long before the layers of sensation created a growing bubble of tension inside her, expanding out and heating up with every slow, deep, deliberate stroke of his cock and every press and slide of his fingers.

Gwen whimpered at the need to come. The need to not have this end before she did. *Please, please, please.* The words chanted in her head with every move.

"Stay with me," Asher murmured again. Almost pleaded.

"I'm here." She moaned at the press of his touch. "I'm close."

So close. She could feel the orgasm starting to gather, to pull in tighter.

"Me too. Hold on, love." She found herself lifted off her side, and he stayed deep inside her as he positioned her on her knees, her upper half still lying in the…

Sand?

Asher, now on his knees behind her, gripped her by the hips and slammed into her, and sand rubbed raw against the side of her face. The realization that she was *definitely* lying on sand almost slipped right out of her head at the sensation of having her body fully possessed like this.

But…sand? In a dream?

"Asher?"

Maybe something in her voice caught his attention, because he slid out to slam back into her—gods that felt so damn good—but then he went dead still.

"Fuck me," he muttered, and not in the voice he was using a second ago. "This is…"

She fisted her hands, digging into the sand, and it felt real. Entirely real. Gritty and raw against her palms and fingers.

Real. This was real.

This wasn't a dream.

Oh. My. Gods.

Shock held her completely and utterly immobile. She was

on her knees with Asher's cock buried inside her and her body screaming for the release they'd been building and chasing.

Together.

And despite what reality meant, she was so damn tempted to tell him to finish first. They could be horrified later.

"Fuck," he snarled again. Then he yanked out of her, leaving her feeling hollowed out and hanging over a drop that would never come.

As if the connection, the tension between them, really had been no more than a distant dream…

CHAPTER ELEVEN

Asher

Asher didn't look at Gwen as he scrambled away and pulled up his fucking pants, giving her enough time and space to get situated. In the tiny area they were crammed into, and given his size, that took some doing.

Ignoring the insistent, unfulfilled throb of his body was even harder with his dragon snarling and pacing in his head, insisting they finish what they started.

But he couldn't do that. Not when he wasn't certain that was what she truly wanted.

When he couldn't stay facing the rock wall any longer without looking like a coward, he turned. "I'm sorry—"

"Don't," she cut him off. Then crossed her arms. "It meant nothing."

She might as well have lanced him in the gut, her words suddenly making it hard for him to breathe. Because under the sharp needle of guilt, Asher still couldn't help but notice the way her cheeks were rosy and her hair mussed. He'd done that. Or the memory of the soft, silky feel of her on his body, around his cock, and the sweet little sounds she'd been making.

He'd made her do that too.

The desperate urge to kiss her until her lips were pink and swollen, to physically brand her as his, grabbed him by the balls and his still hard dick somehow managed to get harder, and he had to take an actual step away, welcoming the jagged rockface digging sharply into his back, to keep from doing exactly what he was picturing. To finish what they'd just been in the middle of.

Mine, his dragon growled.

The fuck she is, Asher growled right back.

Luckily, Gwen didn't seem to notice. She was too busy glaring at him. If she'd been a dragon, fire would have been spitting from her eyes. "Don't you dare apologize. That's worse."

Worse? Didn't she just say it was nothing? "You didn't want…what we were doing." He waved a hand between them. "You never would have let me touch you, let alone—"

"Clearly I would have," she snapped. "I distinctly remember your voice asking me for permission and me giving it. Did I just dream that bit, or did it happen?"

Asher went dead still. "You thought it was a dream?"

The same way he had?

"Yes." She bit the word off like she had a sour taste in her mouth.

Unwillingly, his voice dropped low. "You dream of me often?"

Her lips pressed together in a mulish expression as she looked away with a shrug.

Which meant she did.

Asher ducked his head and grinned, suddenly feeling like

he could crow from the fucking rooftops. All he could think was that in her dreams, once she let herself stop remembering to hate him, she still wanted him.

They both had been dreaming of each other. That had to mean something didn't it?

"Me too."

He could see the moment the implication of that registered with her by the slight widening of her eyes. Humans tended to wave off dreams as random, or a misfiring of neurons, or the brain processing information. But all the creatures of the supernatural world, who were just a little bit more than human, knew better. Dreams were many things: omens, warnings, or a fucking path to a truth you didn't want to admit in waking life.

And he wanted her.

That was his truth. Always had been.

Was it hers too?

Fated. The word whispered through him for the first time since Goran...

Only they couldn't be. He'd determined that the day she'd run from him and hadn't ever come back. A fated mate wouldn't be able to do that. Fate was like gravity, pulling you inexorably closer to the other person, and to be away from them was...

Dragon shifters of great strength and power had been driven to despair by that kind of distance.

Or had the dreams been their link all this time? Is that how he'd survived the loneliness that had often felt like it would crush him.

Was it possible?

Asher could see Gwen was debating how to answer him, and guilt took a few more needles to him for even bringing it up. Because even if there was a truth she didn't want to admit to, it was a conscious decision. He knew that much.

But he couldn't quite make himself change the topic or give her an out, waiting for her move.

Her gaze flicked over his shoulder past him to the entrance to their small shelter, that he now blocked, and the early morning sunlight streaming through it in broken beams. "We need to find water," she said.

Disappointment deflated every hope that had started to fill him up. He was right. She didn't want to want him.

Even so, he wanted to argue. To prod and poke her until…

Until what? Until he broke? Until he died?

If he did that, he'd hurt her a thousand times worse than he already had.

Don't be a bigger asshole than you already are.

He'd respect her boundaries, no matter what. And lying together like that was clearly out now, even for warmth.

She twitched her shoulders, an impatient move she used to do as a girl, so familiar to him that his lips drew up without thinking. Only to stop when she directed a frown his way.

"Listen…we need to survive long enough for you to heal up and be able to fly," she said. "Then we can get the fuck out of here."

She tromped past him and out of the crevice, careful in the small space not to touch him.

"Yeah. Great plan," Asher muttered to himself as he followed her.

Gwen made it all the way to the beach before she stopped and put her hands on her hips, her back to him, staring at the storm clouds raging in the distance. Not nearly as far off as they had been yesterday, maybe one or two islands away. But at least they had a window. A small one probably, as fast as the storm wielder moved.

"Do you think the egg is safe where we left it in the cave while we look for water?" Gwen asked.

Where he'd buried it last night? It'd be as safe as it would anywhere else, including on them, especially if they got caught. They were lucky they hadn't broken it with all the banging around they'd been doing. "Yes."

She nodded, back still to him. "Did any of the plane wreckage find its way to the island with us?"

He knew what she was asking. If they had anything they could use as tools or a bucket. Smart. Gwen had always been smart. "No."

Trapped on a deserted island with more than one thing after them was not the time to be fixing their relationship. They needed to focus on getting to safety, then…maybe…

"Can you fly yet?" he asked by way of distraction.

This would go a hell of a lot faster if she could spot the water and explore the island from the air rather than hiking all over kingdom come.

Asher watched as Gwen fluttered her wings, clamping down on his reaction. She lifted off but only made it a few feet into the air before she dropped back down to the sand with a tiny grunt. Then shook her head. "Not yet. Catching you seems to have done some damage, and I'm still healing."

"Then we explore more on foot like yesterday."

She nodded, then paused. "Where'd our coconuts go?"

He'd dropped his when they'd been running to try to get to shelter before the wraith caught them. She'd probably done the same.

"We need to eat anyway," he said.

Bottling all that inside, he gave one of the slim-trunked trees a great shake using his dragon strength so that four or five coconuts all dropped to the sand.

Making quick work of it like yesterday, he let them both drink the coconut milk and then divvied up the fruits' meat he carved out from the insides for them to eat, then hollowed out the fruit to create vessels for carrying water. Very chewy and fibrous, but at least it was food. "After we get back from looking for water, I'll catch some more fish," he said.

She nodded toward his arm. "I'm surprised you haven't healed yet."

He flexed his right arm, the pain more like a dull ache than anything sharp. That was something at least. "Maybe tomorrow."

"Let's hope," she said, then tucked her wings away and out of sight.

For some odd reason, that small action triggered a memory of the night she'd first learned to fly as a little girl. He'd happened to be there, been privileged to witness the event. Of her parents' twelve children, only Gwen had inherited her mother's moonlight pixie blood, which is why her surname was Moonsoar and not Woodshield, like her father and the rest of her siblings. Including Goran.

"What do your parents think about your job as a courier?"

The question just sort of popped out.

"I wouldn't say they were happy about it. But they understand. They—" Gwen cut herself off like she suddenly realized who she was talking to.

Asher plowed forward anyway. "How are they?"

That got her to look at him, her serious gaze searching his. She tipped her head, then sort of winced, and he knew he wasn't going to like whatever came out of her mouth next.

"Still devastated."

Ouch.

Asher didn't quite hide his flinch, and the way she suddenly leaned back, he knew she'd caught it. He wanted to tell her that he was still devastated, too, because he hadn't just lost a best friend that day, he'd lost the trust and love of people he'd considered family.

And he'd lost her.

But he didn't say any of that. "Ready?"

Her mouth flattened like she was disappointed he didn't argue or defend himself. A shadow of the look she had cast him the day she'd found out about Goran.

Worst day of his life.

She'd begged Asher to tell her it wasn't true, tell her that his part in it wasn't the way he was describing, tell her he was lying. And when he hadn't done any of that, because telling her the truth meant the blood oath would kill him, she'd given him a look of such wretched disappointment, as soon as she'd left the room, he'd vomited the meager contents of his stomach. He'd wanted to run out after her, to ask her not to leave, but he'd known that would only make it worse.

She was gone the next day with no trail and no communication about where she was headed.

"Let her go." The memory of Gwen's father—hollow and pale with his own grief—rattled around in Asher's head. In his heart. *"If you truly care, you won't ever go after her."*

CHAPTER TWELVE

Gwen

Mortified.
That's what Gwen was.

Every step might as well be her own personal torture, not letting her heated, still pulsing flesh calm down from before. Still wanting him was…a big problem.

One she was hoping would just go away on its own.

Asher took the lead through the dense foliage that covered the island, and she was more than happy to follow just so she could deal with her thoughts and her body while not feeling his gaze burning on the back of her neck. Except now the view might just be worse—strong legs, firm ass, broad back covered by a t-shirt that didn't do anything to disguise the ridges of muscles. Memories of his hands on her made fresher by the fact that his hands really had *just* been on her this morning.

The walk wasn't helping calm anything down for her either.

How in heaven's name had she gotten so far down the road of being so thoroughly fucked without waking up sooner?

Because you didn't want to wake up, that voice of truth piped up in her head. *You wanted Asher that badly.*

What was wrong with her?

Her brother was dead because of this man. That should have wiped all traces of history away like a tsunami. Nothing of what they'd been before left in its wake.

Including wanting him.

But the uncomfortably slick, still swollen part of her that twinged with every rotten step, said otherwise.

Screamed it really.

The connection was broken, but she could still feel it haunting her, like the phantom pain of a limb that had been cut off. The nearby storm only made it worse. It was as if the island sensed its nearness and had gone as still as possible. No breeze and the humidity was almost unbearable after all the rain last night.

First thing she was doing when they found water was washing away every trace of her traitorous body's response to Asher.

Maybe then she could stop flushing...and stop thinking about him.

"I think I see something," Asher said, ahead of her.

Gwen carefully composed her features to mild—if still red cheeked—curiosity as he swung around to check where she was.

"This way." He pointed.

It took another five minutes of walking, but his keen dragon eyes hadn't been wrong. They burst out of the denser brush into what amounted to a small clearing around a decent-sized, stream-fed pond. Pristine clear waters that let her see the details of the bottom beckoned, sparkling in the sunlight.

Sweaty from their trek and the feelings that refused to fade, Gwen was damn tempted to dive right in, but before she could, Asher stripped off his shoes and socks, his hands going to the fly of his jeans.

"What are you doing?" she asked.

He didn't face her, but she could hear the rare teasing smile in his voice. "Bathing."

He was going to bathe. Right now? In front of her?

Sure. No big deal. She was a fully grown adult. Most supernatural creatures didn't have hang-ups about nudity the way humans did. She could handle this. He'd go first, then she'd take a turn. They could draw their drinking water upstream when they were done.

Asher dropped his pants, leaving him in nothing but black boxer-briefs, which showed off the muscles of his thighs as he waded into the water. Then he turned to face her, a playful glint in his eyes she hadn't seen in a long time. Sure enough, next came the shirt.

Damn.

There went the small amount of control she'd wrangled for herself over the course of their trek. Gone in an instant.

With an eye roll, she walked to a flat rock at the edge of the water. A second later, a splash told her he was fully submerged now. By the time she'd taken off her socks and shoes, and rolled up her pants to dangle her legs, she figured it was safe for her to look.

A horrible idea, it turned out.

A flash of movement under the surface caught her eye a second before Asher came up out of the water, facing her, lifting his hands to slick back his dark hair, his muscles rippling with the movement.

Godsdamn it. Now that was just freaking unfair.

It was like nature was trying to highlight all the hotness she'd been missing all this time. Hotness that had just been inside of her.

Oh. My. Gods.

Heat flared in her cheeks yet again.

Which was when Asher opened his eyes and caught her staring. His gaze locked in on her, and for once she couldn't make out what he was thinking.

But she couldn't look away, her chest growing tighter by the second.

Was he—

Asher swam toward her. "Why aren't you coming in?"

She nearly shook her head. No, it couldn't be.

Her oh-so-serious dragon wasn't trying to…tease her, play with her?

Was he?

He's not your *dragon, Gwendolyn Moonsoar. He's not your anything,* she tried to remind herself. But that thought was feeling more and more flimsy by the second…considering the way he was looking at her.

She shrugged, trying to play it cool while her face was probably still flaming red. Maybe he'd put that down to their trek? "I'll wait until you're done."

A frown flitted across his features, far more familiar and comfortable than his teasing, but then he swam forward until he could stand in front of her. "You don't have to wait. There's plenty of room."

Gwen opened her mouth to wave him off with something vague only to get a little lost in the deep navy of his eyes. "I… don't think that would be a good idea," she found herself saying.

His jaw tightened visibly. "I would never—"

Without thinking, she pressed a single finger against his

lips and they both sort of froze at the contact. Gwen swallowed and pulled away slowly.

"I know," she whispered. "You're not the one I don't trust."

Asher's brows drew together, stopped, then crept back up as her meaning sank in that *she* was the problem here. Her and all her discombobulated feelings.

That glint from a moment ago reignited in his eyes, only up close it was even more potent, more dangerous. "Do you need rescuing?" he asked, his voice dropping lower.

Oh my gods.

The memory of their first kiss, the first time he'd said those words to her, swirled and blended with this one, and excited butterflies hit her insides full force. But she couldn't.

They couldn't. Could they?

What she wanted to say was, "From you?" like she had back then. Instead, she just shook her head and went to stand up, to put distance between them.

Only Asher grabbed her hand, his hold gentle as she stilled.

"I've missed you, Gwen," he said softly. "I want you to know that."

A lump of emotion and longing formed inside her throat.

Was he *trying* to make this a thousand times harder for her? More confusing? More need-inducing?

When she didn't say anything but she also didn't leave, he slowly moved closer, right up against her rock, so that he was standing between her dangling legs. He paused there. "I really want to kiss you, and not just in a dream, but I won't if you say no, or if you need rescuing for real."

This close, right in her space where she could feel the natural warmth of a dragon shifter radiating from his skin, feel his breath against her cheek…gods, he was temptation.

Gwen forced her gaze away, dropping it to her lap. It didn't help. She still wanted to kiss him. "I—"

She shifted her gaze to the left and paused, then peered closer at his side.

What the—?

Then she choked.

Asher jerked to follow her gaze, searching the water around him for some threat maybe. "What's wrong?"

She stared at him with her mouth ajar for enough time that he stopped searching for danger to bracket her face with his hands, his expression growing harder with concern. "Gwen—"

"I think…" She could hardly make herself say it. "I think you've been poisoned."

CHAPTER THIRTEEN

ASHER

Asher just couldn't get a blasted break on this mission. Or with Gwen.

He sat on Gwen's rock at the edge of the pond, shirt off, with her behind him.

Mostly her fingers flitting over his flesh felt…good. Too good. Her touch was the same as the way she moved—pure sensual grace. Every single one of the grunts he hadn't managed to swallow down had nothing to do with pain. Because he felt no pain. Not even a twinge.

Which explained why he'd had no idea about the poison.

She clicked her tongue. "What about here?"

"Where?"

A small beat of silence, then, "You can't feel this?"

"No."

"That's not good."

"Gwen, so help me gods—"

"I think the poison is numbing you," she rushed to explain. "There's a wound that's black and blue...mostly black...the size of your fist here." She drew a circle, and must've gone outside the boundary of the wound, because *that* he definitely felt.

Asher didn't quite contain another groan and she pulled her hand away sharply.

"Did I hurt you?"

What a question. Asher gritted his teeth. "No."

"Um...okay. Good." She paused, then leaned in closer, inspecting his wound, and his dragon curled up inside him at her nearness.

Then the warmth of her breath feathered across his skin. Fuck. He couldn't do this. "I'll be fine." He nodded toward the dark clouds looming closer that he'd been keeping an eye on. "We need to move soon."

"Oh my gods," she cut him off. "There's a barb in the wound."

Godsdamn that wraith. "Pull it out."

"What if that makes it worse?"

"Just do it—" A grunt tore from him as a shaft of pain, like taking a dragon's barbed tail to the side, stabbed through his back, then radiated outward and up his spine to the base of his skull.

Behind him, Gwen hissed, and he spun around on the rock, thinking she'd pricked herself on the barb, only to find her holding up a nasty looking, curved spike of inky black.

That thing had been *in* him? The wraith must've managed to slip it under one of his scales when they'd been locked in battle midair.

Days.

It had been in him almost two days. Might even explain why he was healing so slowly. Either way, that couldn't be good.

"How bad is it?" he asked.

In answer, Gwen's gaze skittered away from his, the corners of her mouth turning down.

"Gwen?" he prompted.

"I don't want to freak you out, Ash."

He tried very, very hard not to tense at the old nickname. Not to pull her across his lap. She probably didn't even realize she'd called him that.

"*That* bad?" he tried to tease. It came out too serious. He was rusty with teasing.

"Not funny," she muttered, then shoved at his uninjured shoulder to turn him back around. "Whatever that was coated in, it's now in your tissue and blood."

That wiped all attempts at teasing right out of him. "I guess it *is* that bad," he muttered.

"Worse." She sighed. "I assume you've seen a wound with sepsis?"

"Yeah, but not in dragons."

"I don't think it's that. I'm pretty sure I was right the first time, and it's poisoned."

Seven hells. "Describe it."

"Um…Your skin is black around the wound. The poison seems to be visibly spreading up the veins. I can see it under your skin."

Asher glared at the pond which sparkled happily back at him. Fucking wraiths. Damn things were a blight on the world.

"You're going to need a Healer."

She meant a Healer in the supernatural world sense. One lived in Ben Nevis. Enough of Fallon's blood, and Asher'd be all fixed up. But Scotland was a fair flight from Indonesia.

Plus they had to get off this island and get Gwen and the egg to Meilin first.

Maybe Meilin had a Healer?

"Anything you can do to stave it off?" he asked.

"What? Like pixie tricks?" He could practically hear her eyes roll, and his lips twitched again, despite the seriousness of the situation.

Gwen had always had that effect on him.

"You never did convince me pixies don't have secret magic."

"We're not Leprechauns sitting on piles of gold," she said. "Or fae for that matter. We have nature-related powers, stronger in the area our wings designate, and that's all. No extra magic."

"At least Leprechauns or fae could fix me," he grumbled.

Even though he could hear the swipe of her hand coming for the side of his head before she struck, Asher didn't duck. He'd earned that one. Chuckling under his breath, he swallowed it down the next second. He didn't deserve to be teasing her, laughing with her. They were already in a dangerous situation, and now it was worse.

"Let's load up on water and figure me out later." He went to get up only to have her push him gently back down by the shoulder.

"Hold on. I may not have secret magic, but my dad and siblings aren't wood pixies for nothing. They know plants. Stay here a sec" Gwen jumped to her feet and ran off before he could stop her.

"We shouldn't split up," he growled after her, unable to keep the burning need to protect her out of his voice.

Her response floated back to him. "It's daylight. I'm fine."

Something that could turn in a second, as they'd already learned. But before he could point that out, she popped her head around a bush. "I won't go far," she promised, then disappeared again.

Asher counted in his head, willing to give her five minutes at most. But when that came and went with no hint of her return, insidious worry that he had dealt with for thirteen years—every second she'd been out of his sight and out of his life—started to creep in. He was just pushing to his feet to go after her when she reappeared on the other side of the pond. She'd used the bottom of her shirt as a basket to hold what looked like several different types of plants and flowers.

Asher sank back to the rock, trying to look like he'd been bored and not edging toward frantic.

"What were you about to do?" she asked as she hopped over the stream at one end.

He cast about for a reasonable answer. "Fill the coconuts. Might as well get something done while I wait."

"Ah. I need at least one for this anyway," she said as she dropped to her knees in the sand by his rock and started unloading her score onto the ground, lining them up.

"What are you doing?"

"These are all plants with various healing elements—soothing, controlling inflammation, absorbing poison and so on. Ginseng, guava, turmeric, sambiloto—" She pointed to each. "I'm going to make a poultice."

"I see."

Not magic, but still knowledge that she'd picked up from her family. She'd always been a sponge that way.

"Worth a try," she shrugged.

Only he didn't miss the concerned glance she cast toward his back. She wasn't nearly as casual as she was trying to make him believe.

After prepping them in various ways, Gwen layered her ingredients in one of the hollowed-out coconuts, adding a little water from the pond. Then using a rock, she pulverized it all together. She worked diligently, as if he wasn't even there.

For him, pretending she didn't exist was much harder.

Her long, black lashes spread out against her cheeks, and

her tongue kept peeking out between her lips as she concentrated. Asher adjusted his position on the rock, hiding the evidence of his reaction.

Get your shit together.

He should have more self-control than this. That was for damn sure. But he'd never had good control when it came to Gwen.

"No. No control. Claim our mate," his dragon sniped.

Asher ignored his animal side.

"Rip a strip of your shirt off to use as a bandage," Gwen said, still not looking at him.

As distractions went, it was weak, but he'd take what he could get.

They worked in silence until he had a long strip and she stopped pulverizing the mixture. In the quiet, Gwen tilted her head this way and that as she inspected the results.

"I hope it works," she muttered.

"Me too, love."

The endearment slipped out, and Gwen stiffened. Then, in a low voice… "Don't call me that, please."

What was he supposed to say? That calling her love was as natural as breathing fire? That he'd been calling her that in his dreams all this time? That he didn't want to promise that. He'd already promised so many other things that had fucked up his life. Hers, too. "Understood," he said instead.

Not responding, Gwen crawled around behind him with her coconut of gunk and then started layering on the poultice. Other than an ache like pressing on a day's old bruise, and the general sense of something wet and sticky, it didn't feel like much. Certainly not like relief or healing. He wasn't about to tell her that though.

Gwen cleared her throat. "When did you injure your tail?" she asked.

Asher jerked away from her touch, not ready for that question.

"Sorry," Gwen murmured, obviously assuming she'd hurt him with the poultice.

He had to force his muscles to unclench, relaxing back toward her as much as he could. Maybe she'd forget she asked.

"This scar is new," she said. And suddenly a warm finger gently traced the white line of a scar that started at his lower back and ended near his ass crack. "I assume it goes with the tail injury?"

So she wasn't going to give it up. "It does."

Silence settled uneasily between them. Or at least uneasily for Asher. He tried damn hard not to show his own tension. They were getting too close to the truths he wasn't allowed to tell her.

Instead of asking, though, she just waited, the silence growing heavy like the storm hovering in the distance.

Asher debated telling her a lie or maybe a half-truth. But just like thirteen years ago, nothing he could come up with would explain the situation. Nothing but the truth that will kill him to share.

Damn it, Goran.

"You don't want to know, Gwen."

Her hands on his back stopped moving, and he could practically feel the tension building inside her, radiating at him hotter and hotter.

"Are you telling me you were injured when Goran..." She trailed off like she couldn't quite make herself finish the words.

"It's old history," Asher said after a moment.

"Which means yes," she muttered, more to herself than him.

He kept his mouth shut.

After another minute, Gwen continued with her poultice. She said nothing more until she'd applied it all, then stuck a hand out in front of him, ostensibly for the bandage, which he gave her. Only when she went to wrap it around him, she practically plastered herself along his side in the attempt.

Didn't she know she was playing with fire touching him like that? Even platonically. He'd had his cock buried inside her this morning on the strength of a fucking dream.

Asher twitched in her grasp, then sort of wriggled out of her touch. "Let me."

He took the cloth from her hands before she could protest and secured it around himself, feeding the two ends back to her. Once she'd tied it, she got to her feet. He expected her to wash out the coconut, or start filling the unused ones with water, or something.

He didn't expect her to move around to sit on a nearby rock facing him, her chin jutting stubbornly and lips a grim line. "Now that that's done, I want to hear what happened that day."

Fuck.

CHAPTER FOURTEEN

Gwen

Talk to me. Please.

Gwen kept her gaze on Asher's, willing him to finally be honest with her.

All she knew was that, without telling his family, Goran had chosen to help Asher spy. He'd been captured by Thanatos, who'd used him to test Asher's loyalty, and he'd died because of it.

That's not what Asher had said. It's what her family had been told by Thanatos's lackies who'd brought them her brother's ashes.

Asher had told them *nothing*. Not a denial. Not a confirmation. Just...frustrating, immovable silence.

No matter what questions they'd asked.

At first, she hadn't believed it. Couldn't. The way Goran had died, and Asher's involvement went so against who Asher was at his core. She'd all but begged him to tell her

Goran's death hadn't been his fault, but he'd closed off so hard that she'd started to believe that maybe he'd been willing to do anything for his suffering people. He'd never hurt Goran on purpose, but maybe he'd let him die, if he felt he had no choice?

It had been the only thing that made sense at the time.

Still a betrayal of the worst kind.

At that point, she'd plunged so deeply into grief and shock, she hadn't been able to see past the pain.

"Do you really want *details, darling?"* her mother had asked her long ago. *"I'd much rather remember Goran the way he was in life, not the way he died. I don't want those images in my head."*

Gwen had dropped it then. Hell, she'd run.

And maybe that had been wrong.

Hells, she'd love to be in the wrong if it meant she'd misjudged the man staring back at her now. That, at least, was something she could try to right, that they could work through.

But he was fucking doing it again. Stonewalling her. Refusing to tell her anything.

A fact that had pissed her off then. The burn of it lingered in her veins, in her heart, in everything she did. Now it stoked hotter with every beat.

She was going to get the truth, damn it.

Because if Asher had been injured trying to help her brother, that told a very different story about Goran's death than the one she knew.

After a long beat, Asher got to his feet. "We can't stay here."

As if it was helping make his point, a loud rumble of thunder crawled across the sky. She glanced over her shoulder and jumped to her feet. Seven hells, whatever drove that storm was strong. And fast. It was looming over them.

"We better hurry." Asher grabbed a coconut, scooping up

water, and guzzling it down. Then he grabbed another to toss to her. "Drink up."

Gwen caught the tossed coconut husk with ease but instead of doing like he said, she sat staring.

Staring...and waiting.

"It's history, Gwen," he finally said in a voice that carried a finality that hit her heart wrong. He was hurting. He'd never admit it, but now, without the immediacy of her own grief blinding her, she could see it. But he wouldn't fix it.

Why? She wanted to scream it at him. Beg him.

"It's *my brother's* history," she insisted. "I deserve to know."

He refused to look at her, jaw working, the muscles so twitchy under his skin she was surprised his teeth weren't breaking. "No."

Asher didn't so much as glance in her direction again as he drank down at least three more coconuts full. The man was probably dying of thirst after everything he'd done to get them to the island and then taking care of her while she slept. Plus, he was big, and poisoned, and injured.

And the storm was hunting them. And getting close.

Which was the only reason why she started to fill the coconuts, setting them side by side on the sandy spit of beach. They gathered their water, and started off toward their crevice, walking quite a ways. But she couldn't let it go.

"If you don't tell me," she aimed the words at his back. "I'll ask your king."

Asher paused mid-step, six-foot-four frame rigid for a half a second before he put his head down, barreling ahead through the brush. "Go ahead," he said. "He wasn't there."

Frustration and all the years of pent-up anger singed her insides.

Tell me, damn you. Why was he making this so hard on both of them? There had to be a reason. "King Ladon may not have been there, but I have no doubt he knows more than you've shared."

"And he'll ask me before he tells you any of it." He tossed her a grimly smug look over his shoulder. "I'm his beta."

Yeah. She'd heard that. After all, in her line of work for Delilah, she had her ear to the ground about most of supernatural kind.

Asher was the blue dragon king's second-in-command. In line for the throne should the king, or his offspring, fail to continue their line.

"You've come up in the world," she murmured. "Spy. Murderer." She watched him closely for a reaction to that word, but it didn't come. "And now—"

"His Viceroy of War."

"Ah." That she hadn't known. Dragon kings tended to keep their Curia Regis, or king's council, fairly secret. But Asher had always been a fighter. Even as a kid, he'd had a natural talent for it. So it wasn't exactly a surprise.

"Ladon is a friend," Asher said now. "So is Skylar, his queen."

Friend. Asher had friends. Friends that weren't Goran.

The old bitterness she'd carried around for more than a decade prompted her to wonder if *they* knew what he'd done to her brother? What friendship meant to this man?

Except nothing was fitting together, like she was trying to assemble a puzzle with pieces from different boxes. This time, though, she wasn't letting it go. She wasn't going to keep running. Not anymore. "I'm going to find out the truth, Asher. One way or another."

His body pulled drawstring tight, like a bow at its zenith, ready to loose a deadly arrow. But instead of yelling, or throwing the coconut in his hand, Asher only let out a long, pent-up breath.

"You want to believe I'm not the bad guy," he said. "That's

why you're still asking these questions." He stopped and faced her abruptly, pinning her with burning, blue-flamed irises. "Let me save you the trouble. I *am* the bad guy in your story. Stop digging."

She stared at him, every part of her rejecting those words hard. Even with the lingering anger and confusion and blame, deep down she knew he wasn't that.

He banked the flames showing in his eyes, and for a moment, she swore she could see the smoke rising from the embers. He took off again, shoulders slightly rounded like he'd given up.

Asher never gave up. On anything. The man was the walking definition of determined.

He wasn't going to put her off. Not this time.

"I'm digging anyway."

Asher's brows lowered, his expression darkening, though with the way he turned his back to her, she almost missed the pain dragging at his features. "I can't, Gwen."

The resignation in his voice, in the slight hunch to his shoulders was painfully obvious. But it was the word "can't" that had her stilling.

Can't.

Not won't.

He'd never said that before. He'd never said he couldn't.

"Why not?" she asked.

He straightened, regret disappearing behind stoic acceptance. "I just can't. And anyone else who knows the truth is dead."

CHAPTER FIFTEEN

Gwen

They'd barely made it back to their crevice before the storms rolled in again. Hard.

Every flash of light came with an immediate clap of thunder so violent she imagined the entire island shook with the force.

Clearly the wraith—or wraiths if that's what they were dealing with—and its electricity-prone helper were dead set on getting the damn egg, still buried safely in their crevice.

Another *flash, boom* rocked the tiny cave where they'd holed up.

"That was close," she murmured, not turning her head, but aiming the words toward where Asher was lying.

They'd been here all afternoon and now into the night, and she was on first watch.

Gwen had spent the time weaving together large leaves that she'd collected on their walk back into what amounted to blankets and pillows. Good thing they'd gotten water. But even so, her stomach was a grumbling mess after only coconut to eat earlier in the day.

Flash. Boom.

Gwen flinched. Was it getting…closer? She'd figured it was right on top of them.

Sitting near the entrance with her back propped against the jagged-edged rock wall, protected by her leaf pillow, and with her leaf blanket over her lap, she leaned forward, focused. Heart in her throat, she carefully watched the lightning illuminating beyond the entrance of the cave, searching the roiling sky for any sign of the wraith.

Hours. They had hours before daylight could drive the wraith away again. That was if the storm gave up searching the island where they hid.

Gwen dropped her head back against the rock wall. It was going to be a long night.

"No—"

Asher's voice reached to her in the darkness, but she hadn't said anything. Frowning, she cocked her head, listening. Did he need something?

"Don't make me promise that."

Gwen stilled.

"Not that," he said again.

Not what? Promise what? They hadn't talked promises. He couldn't be talking about what was happening to them here.

Sitting straighter, she looked toward where he lay about six feet away. It was too dark to see him, though. "Ash?" she whispered.

With the wraith so close, they'd agreed. No talking. No noise. No movement. No fire. Nothing that could attract even the smallest amount of attention.

"I understand," he muttered. The dejection in his voice. The resignation.

Her heart squeezed, even as realization struck. He had to be talking in his sleep. Not a very trained fighter thing to do, which ratcheted up her worry. Was the poison making him sick?

"Asher?"

A flash of lightning lit up just enough of their hiding spot to see him, lying on his side with his back to her. He twitched with a grunt.

Then the light was gone.

Should I wake him?

Gwen didn't move.

Another flash of lightning, only this time, Gwen caught the violent trembling of Asher's body.

It wasn't that cold in here. Not with their makeshift blankets.

And dragons didn't suffer sickness. This had to be the poison. Was he delirious?

Gwen was kneeling next to him before she even thought to move. A hand to his shoulder confirmed he was still fast asleep. He stirred slightly at her touch but didn't wake.

"Asher?" She gave him a shake.

A groan, a move away from her hand, but still out.

She leaned over him, putting a hand to his forehead, before she hissed at the feel. He was icy to the touch. Dragons always ran hot. Only severe sickness could creep past their natural healing and turn them cold like this.

And when they lost their fire…

"No. No. No," she muttered under her breath as she moved blanket, shirt, and bandage out of her way.

She had to wait again for another flash of lightning, because Asher was further into the cavern. The illumination was dimmer here when it came, but that didn't matter. The ugly blackish-purple tendrils of poison had crawled all the way up to his shoulder blade, and as she pulled his pants back, down his leg just as far as she could see.

"Gods above," she whispered, her voice suddenly hoarse.

A frantic, unfamiliar sort of panic set in at the sight. And for the first time since he'd shown up, tackling the wraith midair, the truth struck at her.

Cleaved her in two.

I still love him.

In truth, she had never stopped, even when she hadn't let herself think of him. Feel anything for him. Even when she was so angry with him that she wanted to never see him again.

Seven hells.

But what if the truth she was going to try to uncover didn't change any of that?

Gods… she didn't know what she would do if that ended up happening. She needed this damned stubborn, secretive, grumpy dragon shifter like she needed moonlight. More. She could live without him, but only truly felt alive with him. Always had.

She just hadn't let herself admit it or feel it. Except in her dreams.

What did that mean for them moving forward?

She couldn't say, yet. But if he died before they had a chance to figure it out…

"Don't die on me now," she pleaded with his unresponsive form. "Not when I need you. Not when I…"

Her throat closed around the words.

Another flash of lightning and thunder hit along with a pelting of sideways rain coming through the crack. It felt like the storm was trying to crawl in here with them.

Asher groaned in his sleep. A sound of torment.

Scrambling by feel alone to the corner of their hidey hole,

she found the coconuts, most filled with water, one filled with prepped plants of her poultice. All she needed to do was grind them up with a little water.

It took several more flashes to check her work before she was satisfied. Then she was back at Asher's side again, rolling him over, washing off the wound with water before applying more poultice. It hadn't done much before, but there was nothing else she could think to do.

And doing nothing sucked.

How could such a strong body give into darkness like this? She'd always thought of Asher as indestructible.

Tying the bandage back over it, she was mid-pull on the ends to tighten it when another flash illuminated something she hadn't noticed before.

"What the—"

Gwen leaned her face closer to the top of his wound, and the black tendrils rising out of the top of the bandage. In the dark, she couldn't see a darn thing, so she had to wait once more. This time, as soon as the flash came, she deliberately pressed a finger into his flesh and then, holding the pressure, traced one of the tendrils. Sure enough, the inky poison moved inside him like liquid.

No.

Not liquid. Like *shadow*.

Like darkness.

That claw embedded in him had been a piece of the wraith. Asher was being poisoned with *darkness*.

Gwen jerked up straight, staring down at the man she still loved, suddenly knowing what she had to do.

Light was the only thing that could make the darkness go away, but she had drained herself of moonlight when she'd lured the wraith away from Asher, and she hadn't been given an opportunity to absorb more.

This time, the boom came at the same exact time as the flash, and Gwen flinched.

They're so close. I should wait.

Wait for the storm to at least get farther away before she tried what she was thinking.

She rolled Asher to his back, wincing when he groaned in pain. "Sorry," she whispered as she laid over the top of him. Yes, putting more pressure on the wound, but the sand would help his back side retain a little heat. Gwen pulled both leaf blankets up over them, and then wrapped herself around him, trying to get as much contact with his torso as possible.

It would be better for them to be skin to skin, but she needed to be ready the second she got a chance to go.

Goosebumps chased across her skin in shivers at the icy feel of his neck against her forehead. His shaking was violent enough to rattle her a bit. Like lying on a giant vibrating bed. His teeth took up chattering, clicking away above her head, but her ear was pressed over his heart, and the beat there was strong. Rapid. Too fast. But strong.

"Hold on just a little bit longer," she whispered.

The storm outside raged, sending sheets of water into the entrance of their cavern. The booms and flashes crashed into the island over and over in a simultaneous battering that seemed never ending.

Gwen kept her gaze glued on the only way in and out, expecting with every flash to see a shadow figure crawling inside. Coming for them.

She pressed herself to Asher, and continued to listen to his heart, and prayed while she waited for her chance.

"She hates me..." Asher groaned these words like they pained him, his voice a blurred echo inside the cavity of his chest against her ear.

Gwen frowned but didn't lift her head. He was delirious.

Besides...he didn't necessarily have to be talking about her. They'd been apart a long time. There had to have been other women in his life.

Blinding jealousy, apparently, was like fire in the veins, and she didn't deserve to feel it, but she did. Even though she'd walked away.

"She hates me," he muttered. He thrashed his head to the side. "Gwen hates me." His voice choked around the words as if they were worse than the shadows poisoning his blood. As if that knowledge poisoned his heart. His soul.

"...hates...me..."

Flash. Boom.

Almost like the violence of the storm had struck him directly, Asher took three, rapid, harsh breaths, and then sort of shuddered before going so still, she choked. His body was dead weight under her.

"No," she growled the word. "You won't die on me. Not tonight. We have too much ahead of us, and you need to be here for it."

She tucked her head to his chest, pressing her ear tight to him, and her breath escaped in a pent-up whoosh. His heart was still beating.

But barely.

Asher's pulse had turned threadbare, almost impossible to hear, his chest barely moving.

The storm was still raging overhead, no further away, but she couldn't wait. Not any longer.

Asher was going to die if she didn't try something now.

"Trust me to save you," she whispered in his ear. "I'm coming right back."

Gwen threw herself off his body and to her feet and grabbed a weapon Asher had fashioned which lay in the sand by the coconuts. She burst out of their cavern and, unfurling her wings, which immediately turned heavier in the rain, took off into the skies.

Her right wing and back muscles screamed at her for the sudden effort, not fully healed. And between that and the winds and rain knocking her around, she had to push hard. But she would do whatever it took to save Asher.

Keep going.

Inch by inch by inch she gained altitude, moving higher until finally she touched the bottoms of the clouds. Doing her best to not get tossed around, she beat her wings, which thanks to the deluge of rain grew more and more heavy with every beat. Pixies could fly in a light rain shower, but this was like getting dunked in the ocean, like lifting cement. Any second they'd stop working and she'd drop like a rock. But she didn't stop.

She couldn't.

Keep going. Keep—

Something slammed into her from the side, tackling them both so they flipped end over end as they grappled through the skies. Gwen didn't hesitate. Not struggling in its grasp to get away, but instead turning in toward it.

She was close enough to see the wraith's glowing eyes widen in the recess of its hood when she dragged the talon the fucker had left in Asher across where it's abdomen should be, gutting the damn thing, or so she hoped.

The wraith reared back, its scream more like a whistle, piercing her ear before it disappeared. Entirely. Here, holding her, screaming at her, then gone. Like smoke in the wind.

Gwen fluttered her leaden wings, hovering there for a second. "What in the seven hells?"

Then lightning illuminated a sky that sent horror cleaving through her like a scythe.

Oh my gods.

It took every teeth-gritting ounce of courage in her not to fly for safety.

It's not just one.

Maybe at the beginning they had been dealing with one wraith, but like sharks scenting blood in the water, the thing had help now. And the skies were filled with…at least a thirty of the fuckers.

Hanging in midair. Hovering.

Every single eerie hooded gaze trained directly on her.

CHAPTER SIXTEEN

*G*WEN

Get above the clouds. Now.
Gwen shot straight up in the sky, gritting her teeth with every flutter of wings that didn't want to work as she tried to outrun a pack of wraiths made of shadow.

She didn't get far.

One showed up in her path, reaching for her with those otherworldly hands that were somehow both shadow and flesh. She spun out of reach and angled away and up. But another grabbed her by the long, bottom loop of her injured wing.

It broke off with a wild flare of pain that dragged a scream out of her, but she could still fly. That was the purpose of that loop. A lure for predators.

She got maybe twenty feet higher before another one grabbed her wing fully and she jerked up so hard, the agony that tore through her was like glass through flesh. *Fuck!* Her wing had ripped this time. She wouldn't be able to fly.

But the tops of the clouds—the moonlight—was so close.

"No!" she yelled.

Asher.

The word broke apart in her throat as she was yanked against a body that wasn't solid but clutched her tightly all the same. The wraith's hold was like ropes, pinning her arms and her wings to her body. She immediately shimmered her wings away to avoid more damage, even as she kicked at another wraith that appeared in front of them, reaching for her.

"Get off me!" she yelled.

More wraiths closed in, every strike of lightning a dreadful flash on their cloaked bodies. They were coming from every angle she could see, eyes aglow in the dark recesses of their tatty hoods. Panic wrapped around her heart and ribs and squeezed, trying to cut off her breathing.

This is what bloodthirsty looked like on a wraith.

Terror sent ice through her blood.

But she refused to beg.

"I don't even have the damn egg. It's down there—"

A shadowed hand clamped over her mouth. Or maybe not a hand, because the thing holding her was still using two arms. The smell of sulphur blended with a metallic taste against her tongue, making it hard to breathe.

Why didn't they want her to speak? To know where the egg was hidden? Wasn't that what they had come for?

The wraiths closed in, and darkness cut off her sense of sight. Like being swallowed. Like nothing existed in the world except the shadowy hands reaching for her. Terror tried to claw through her, managing to paralyze her for several seconds, but the need to fight kicked in hard, and she tried to thrash in their hold.

Gwen clawed and bit and scratched and kicked.

But she might as well have lain still and accepted her death for all the good it did.

She swore between gusts of wind, and the wraith holding her chuckled in her ear. A scratchy sound, otherworldly. She jerked away from it, revulsion turning her stomach.

This is it.

It's over.

Asher was dying, and she couldn't save him now.

They'd squandered the second chance the fates had given them.

She'd squandered it.

For nothing.

"Meet me in the afterlife," she sent the thought careening toward him.

Maybe there they'd be able to start over with fresh hearts and fresh eyes.

"When I give...the signal...drop."

At the deep, thready voice tiptoeing around in her head, Gwen jolted against the wraith binding her. *"Asher?"*

Gods his voice was barely audible, and not because of the raging storm.

He was awake? He was...here?

She looked around frantically like she couldn't see out of the godsforsaken darkness. *"Don't try to fly when they let you go,"* he said.

Suddenly, a roar shattered even the storm's fury, and blue flames slammed into the wraiths, the heat immediately so intense, she felt flash boiled. Luckily, the wraiths were thick enough around her that the fire didn't touch Gwen.

Or it had nothing to do with luck. Asher had learned impressive control in the last decade.

The wraith holding her let go, its whistling screams joining the others. Somehow, either being frozen with shock or her body obeying Asher's order, Gwen dropped below the fray. She didn't fly. Instead, she looked up in time to see the massive navy-colored dragon—appearing black in the darkness—as it looped away from the wraiths, taking out two or three of the shadowed monsters with a swipe of his half-barbed tail.

At the same time, he used the fire spewing from his maw with impressive precision, targeting wraith after wraith and hitting them dead on.

All in the seconds she fell away.

Gods, he was incredible.

All it took was those few moments to see the hunter he was. The warrior he had become. And for the smallest beat of time, hope cut like a knife through the fear, and she thought that maybe they could get through this.

Except when he went to turn, stretching out his right wing with a maneuver he was clearly used to doing, it buckled under the strain of the turn. That arm still not healed.

The wraiths saw their opportunity and descended on him like a swarm of vampires.

Still falling, Gwen reached a hand toward Asher as his indigo head rose like a serpent above the thrashing wraiths attacking him, mouth open in a silent roar.

"No!" Gwen screamed.

Before she could unfurl her wings and try to help him, a brownish green dragon claw scooped her out of the air.

"Don't worry, little pixie. I've got you," an unfamiliar voice drawled in her head. One with an Australian lilt to the words.

She didn't know this guy, but she had to assume he was here at Meilin's orders. "Help him!" she yelled, pointing up to the skies where the roiling storm had closed the clouds around Asher and the wraiths. "Help my mate!"

CHAPTER SEVENTEEN

Gwen

"They've got Asher covered, sweetheart." The green dragon hitched his chin off to the right and Gwen followed his gaze only to gasp.

Dragons. At least twenty of them. Two blues in the lead of multiple greens of all shades and shapes and sizes, and at least one red in the mix.

They shot through the skies like deadly arrows.

As one, the dragons opened their fiery maws and roared their challenge.

As if the storm itself—or whatever was controlling it—tucked tail and ran, the lightning and thunder stopped abruptly, quickly retreating.

Some wraiths flew away immediately, their dark shadows like holes in the clouds and then gone. Gwen couldn't see what happened with the others. Sitting in the curled talon of the green dragon that carried her, peering between its digits like cage bars, she couldn't see the fight going on above them. All she could do was listen, the roars of dragons battering her ears. The skies, instead of lighting with electricity, flashed with dragon fire reflecting off the clouds around her. Green. Blue. Red.

But she didn't care about any of that.

She was watching.

For Asher to fall from the sky. How he'd woken up at all, let alone healed enough to get up here to help her was a damned miracle. But no way could he have held off the wraiths without burning through whatever stubborn reserves he'd tapped into.

He'd need to truly heal this time, and soon.

"Asher," she whispered to herself.

And maybe she thought it loudly enough for the dragons to pick up on, because a vaguely familiar voice—like gravel—sounded in her head. *"We have him."*

They had him.

He wouldn't fall to his death.

The relief that swept through her was sharp and sweet, only to immediately dull with realization.

"Get me above the clouds," she ordered the dragon who still had her.

"No can do, pixie woman. I have orders—"

"Asher's been poisoned by a shadow wraith. I need to absorb moonlight to try to save him."

A beat of silence in her head. Then, *"Understood."*

With a great beat of his wings that stirred the clouds around them, the dragon lifted them up and up and up until they burst through the cloud tops, which were slowly dissipating.

In the pristine, clear skies, Gwen felt the sheer moonlight all around her. Like a fizzing excitement under her skin. In her blood.

The instant those cool rays hit her, Gwen started to glow.

Faintly at first.

Then bright and brighter as she tipped her face to the majesty of the light that fed her power. "Hello, mistress," she greeted the crescent orb in the sky.

The moon never answered, but Gwen had talked to her since she was a little girl. She considered them to be friends.

"Should I let you go?" the dragon asked.

"I broke my wing."

"So no."

"I'll climb up, if I may."

He loosened his grip on her. *"Be my guest."*

Out from the shadow of the massive dragon's hold, the moonlight struck her fully—sweet, cool, and effervescent. Like swimming in the pure waters of the stream-fed pond they'd found on the island. Gwen reveled in it as she climbed, even as she urged her body to take it in faster. The glow surrounding her, emanating from her very core through her skin, through her soul, burned brighter and brighter and brighter.

"Well fuck me sideways." The dragon she was now seated on the back of murmured the words almost reverently. *"Never seen anything like that."*

"Don't look at me directly," she urged.

"I'm not a novice," he grumbled back.

She would have chuckled if her mind wasn't entirely with Asher. He was already so sick before she'd left him in the cave.

After fighting the wraiths...

"Hold on a little longer," she urged him. *"I'm coming. I'm coming."*

She held out, absorbing as much as she could. If she needed more, she'd come back, but quickly getting her light into Asher's body to fight the shadows was more important. Everything inside her cried out to get to him fast.

Like her soul was tied to his and knew.

Knew that he was almost gone.

She couldn't wait any longer.

"Take me to him," she urged.

"Yes, ma'am." The green dragon tipped over in a fluid slide, tucking his wings in tight, taking them straight down in a breath-snatching, wind-rushing, almighty blur of motion.

Gwen held on tight to the spike she sat behind, then sort of grunted and groaned at the same time when he flared his wings, pulling them sharply to a halt just in time to touch his feet down. She rocked with his body through the landing, then again as he dropped to his belly, allowing her to climb off.

She didn't have to ask where to go.

The group of four men and one woman gathered around a prone form on the ground was impossible to miss.

So was the odd sense of knowing settled dead center in her chest.

She could *feel* Asher.

Only mates could do that, and usually only after they'd mated, and their bond settled into place.

Gwen didn't bother with niceties. "Let me through." She shoved her way past several broad-shouldered giants, men who were about as immovable as mountains. But they moved for her until she was in the inner circle, where she dropped to her knees at Asher's side.

At the sight of his face, fear took a tight grip of her heart, threatening to rip it out.

He looked…terrible.

Not just pale, but gray. And waxy.

Like a corpse.

He wasn't moving. As far as she could tell, he wasn't

breathing.

"No," she whispered.

I can't be too late. I can't.

Not after what they'd both gone through to get here.

"Are you the courier?" the man kneeling on his other side asked.

Gwen didn't answer, putting her ear to Asher's heart instead. Nothing. She held her breath and willed her own heart to stop beating so damn loud. She needed to hear.

Still nothing.

No movement.

No sound.

"Don't die," she begged him. "Don't die on me now. We haven't had enough time."

"I guess the courier knows him," a more feminine voice murmured from behind her.

Thump. Asher's heart thudded hard enough for her to feel it against her face. Like the only part of him still alive was reaching for her.

Gwen gasped and jerked her head up. "He's still alive. Help me roll him over."

"Roll him over?" the man asked. "Why?"

"Just do it."

"Ladon, listen to her." This from the woman again.

Ladon. Asher's king and friend. A fact she brushed aside as she started pushing at Asher's solid form on the ground, only to have the man shoo her out of his way and turn Asher's body over with little strain.

Gwen pulled Asher's shirt up and yanked off the bandage, wiping away the remains of the poultice.

Ladon hissed between his teeth, a sharp sound of shock and realization all in one, and around them the dragon shifters all stiffened or shuffled. They had to know with a single glance how bad this was. Worse, even, than only minutes ago—had it only been minutes—before she'd flown out of their hiding spot.

"What is that?" Ladon demanded in a low growl that was pure royal fury.

"Shadows from a wraith," she said as she closed her eyes. "Poison."

"Can you fix it?"

"I damn well intend to try." Then she cut off everything around her—all her senses focused inward, no longer hearing or feeling anything. Seeing only the moonlight gathered inside her like a tank.

Not full.

Not even half full. There hadn't been time.

Please let it be enough.

Gwen breathed and sent a prayer up to the elders, who existed in everything around her. She breathed and focused on her magic. Not cold like the moonlight, but warm, like Asher's campfires. Like his skin against hers.

His lips.

The way he looked at her.

She took her time.

She had no choice, even as dread and worry clawed at her to hurry.

Halfhearted magic was worse than no magic at all. It could do the opposite of what you were intending. Her mother's words, her training, whispered through her mind.

Do it right the first time, or don't do it at all.

So she went through every detail of the painstaking ritual.

Focus. Gather. Breathe.

She unfurled her wings, spreading them wide, ignoring the pain of where she was broken.

Focus. Gather. Breathe.

She moved her hands in the air around her in a dance

only known to moonlight pixies, a series of flowing moves that both told a story but also drew out her magic.

Focus. Gather. Breathe.

Next, she pulled the light from inside her into the palms of her hands, the warmth of her power protecting her from the cold of the light.

Focus. Gather. Breathe.

She physically pushed the light into Asher's wound, a dark mark her magical eyes could sense even with her physical eyes closed.

The darkness resisted.

Stuffing down panic, she pushed harder, breathing through her anxiety, holding onto the calm, onto the magic, with everything she had.

Then the shadows gave way, just a little, and the light pushed inside.

"Fuck me," Ladon murmured. "You seeing this?"

Gwen didn't look.

Focus. Gather. Breathe.

She pushed even more light into Asher's body. The darkness gave a little easier this time, but too much of it was still inside him. The stain was still there.

More light.

This time, when she pushed, he twitched. She saw it behind her eyelids in the way the light and shadows sort of shimmied.

Is it working? Or am I killing him?

Maybe she was filling him with competing forces that warred with each other and tore his already sickening body apart.

No. The shadows will kill him for sure if I don't do this, she reassured herself.

Focus. Gather. Breathe.

More light.

He grunted this time.

More light.

She was almost out.

A groan, long and drawn out, and his body arched, like he was trying to chase her touch, the sound he was making something closer to pleasure.

"Fuck," Ladon muttered, then, "You're killing him."

He reached for her, hands grasping her wrists and she batted him away. "He's dead if I don't."

More light.

Gwen was breathing hard by now.

This better do it, because as she gave one final push of light, she was out. That was everything.

Asher's body went deathly still beneath her touch.

Gwen opened her eyes and her stomach pitched at the sight of a black, tar-like substance oozing out of his now glowing wound.

"Roll him to his side," she said. "With the wound down."

Thank the gods they listened, not bothering with questions.

"Is it draining?" she asked, sitting in front of Asher's front.

"Yes." Ladon made a face. "But I don't think it's helping—"

Gwen put her ear to Asher's chest again.

No beat. Not that she could hear.

No sound at all.

No movement.

Just…nothing.

Something inside her broke. Snapped clean through. He was a dragon. Dragons were indestructible.

Nothing ever hurt him.

Except me.

She grabbed his hand, gripping it with both of hers and put her ear to his chest. "Don't go," she whispered, her voice cracking around the words. "Don't leave me here alone."

CHAPTER EIGHTEEN

Asher

Consciousness came to Asher slowly. As if he was emerging not from sleep but from a dreamless sort of darkness that felt...cloying, like fingers were trying to drag him down. Keep him down.

Groggy.

That was the word for it.

Hells, even his dragon felt heavy, like they'd both been sedated.

I'm never groggy. A warrior had to be able to go from a dead sleep to on his feet fighting without missing a beat.

So he fought the dark that wanted to keep him under and pushed his way up. The first thing to hit his senses was the beeping of machines. Then the feel of a bed. The sheets soft on his skin. Soft was wrong. Why was soft wrong?

He frowned as he peeled his eyes open.

To light.

Warm light that followed the seams where the rock walls of the room he was in met the ceiling.

I'm in a dragon mountain.

That much was clear. Not his room, though. Sure, his was barely personal, just a place to sleep and sometimes eat, but it wasn't this sparse.

And nothing beeped in there.

Asher turned his head slowly, wincing at the way that made the room sway like palm trees on an island.

Palm trees.

He frowned harder.

Something about an island.

The sight of machines at his bedside interrupted that thought. Machines that were monitoring…

Me.

Hooked up to him and measuring heart rate and blood pressure and so on. An I.V. line trailed down to his arm. Another line leading under the covers. That explained the slightly uncomfortable pressure in his dick.

Not the fun kind.

"You're awake!" a gravely male voice said with…Was that relief underpinning the unusually dead steady tone?

Ladon.

His king.

His friend.

A sound of a chair scraping back across rock, and then a scarred face with dragon blue eyes hovered over him.

"You fucking catheterized me?" Asher growled.

Rather than take offense, Ladon grinned. "Technically *I* didn't. Fallon did the dirty work."

Fallon? The slowly clearing fog in his brain told him something had gone terribly wrong. He just couldn't remember what.

He gritted his teeth, searching the blankness that was his memories.

Ladon grinned. "Nice to have you back with the living, brother."

How long had he *not* been with the living?

"What happened?"

"What do you remember last?" Ladon asked.

Asher tried the think, but it tweaked the ache in his head to do that. The fog was more of a mist now, but still slowing him down. "Meeting with Meilin," he said slowly. "Is that where we are?"

No. Ladon said Fallon was treating him. That meant he was in Ben Nevis in Scotland.

"We're home," Ladon said, confirming that train of thought. He paused. "We were at Yulong Xueshan." Home base for the green dragons. That much he knew. "You remember Delilah?"

He knew the woman, but... "Was she at Yulong Xueshan?"

Why?

"No." Ladon shook his head. "You went to find one of Delilah's couriers who'd gone missing."

Courier.

A flash of an achingly familiar face, pale and determined, inside the cockpit of a plane surrounded by storm.

Gwen.

Asher jackknifed in the bed, sitting straight up as everything came back with a rush that threatened to knock him back under.

He swayed with the motion, and Ladon lurched forward, a hand at his back. "Whoa there. What's the rush?"

"Where is she?" His dragon snarled, frantic and struggling with the fog in his head.

Ladon frowned. "Who?"

"Gwen."

"The courier?" Ladon asked slowly, like he wasn't quite keeping up.

Panic threatened to crush Asher, the weight of it like a thousand boulders on his lungs. "At least tell me she's alive."

"She's fine."

Thank the gods.

"Saved your ass, actually. The egg too."

Who gave a shit about the damn egg?

Asher sank back against the pillows. "I need to talk to her."

He'd known when he'd used the last of his strength to blast those wraiths off her that if they survived, they couldn't go on like they had been. That he'd have to find a way around his oath to Goran. That or die.

Either way, he was going to tell Gwen everything. At least she'd know the truth. That was better, wasn't it? Better than this limbo they were stuck in because of a promise he gave in blood and the way Goran's death made things look.

Ladon's eyes narrowed, still oblivious. "She's gone."

Another growl from his dragon. This one threatening their friend. Asher didn't even blink or bother to leash the beast inside him. "The fuck you mean gone?"

"We got both of you, and the egg, to Meilin. What Gwen did with her light got the poison out of you. Meilin's Healer was able to do a little more, so we knew you'd live. Gwen left Yulong Xueshan as soon as she knew you were going to be all right. After that we brought you here."

Asher sank back against the pillows. She'd run. Again. Escaped him.

And when a moon pixie didn't want to be found…

Fuck.

"Get me unhooked now."

He had to find her. Had to tell her.

Ladon pushed a button that rang a bell somewhere, and

in seconds Fallon was in the room. The grim set of his features lifted when he saw Asher. "You're awake! Thank the gods!"

"And pixies..." Ladon muttered.

"Get me unhitched from all this," Asher tugged on his I.V. line. "I need to go."

Fallon cast Ladon a questioning glance. "I don't advise—"

Asher threw back his covers, grabbing the catheter line. "I will rip this out. I swear to the gods—"

"Stop! I'll do it." Fallon bolted to the bed. "Seven hells, Ash, that's not a good idea."

It would've probably been some of the worst pain he'd ever experienced, but dragons healed. His dick would've been fine.

Find her, his dragon snarled.

Asher was in total agreement. He had a narrow window to find his pixie before she went so far underground, he'd probably have to wait a hundred years for her to pop back up on any radar, let alone his.

The minutes it took for Fallon to release him from all the tubes and beeping felt almost as long as the minutes it had taken him to fly up to where Gwen was being overrun by wraiths in that godforsaken storm.

As soon as he was able, Asher was out of the bed and down the hall on wobbly legs that really did not want to work right. Ladon waved Fallon off but followed himself. All the way to Asher's rooms, where he dressed quickly in jeans and a t-shirt, then threw a pack on the bed and started stuffing it with clothes and gear.

"You're as weak as a newborn bird. Where do you think you're going in this state?" Ladon demanded, arms crossed as he leaned against one wall, watching.

Asher whirled to face him, going military straight, shoulders back, feet at ninety degrees. "Respectfully, my king, I would like to tender my resignation as Beta, Viceroy of Defense, and captain of your king's guard. Effective immediately."

Ladon's eyes widened, flaring with blue fire. It was a rare display of shock from the man. He came sharply off the wall with a growl. "What?"

Asher gave him a single imploring look of apology, then went back to packing.

"Denied," his king snapped.

His dragon snorted in his head.

"You can't deny me this." Asher didn't bother to stop what he was doing.

The king would calm down eventually. Skylar would make sure of that. Although she might be just as pissed and flabbergasted as her mate to start with.

"I can and I will deny it until you give me a damn good reason why—"

"She's my fated mate."

About time you figured that out.

He didn't stop his packing, ignoring the dead quiet that settled between them in the room. "I have to find her before she disappears again."

"Again…" Ladon murmured. "You've got to give me more than that, brother." The words were quiet enough, but the command still lingering in them was unmistakable.

"You remember Goran?"

Ladon didn't respond for a few seconds, frowning. "The go-between who delivered your intel to me when you were in deep undercover with Thanatos?"

"Yeah."

"A pixie," Ladon said this more to himself, his sharp mind already headed down the right turns to the truth.

"He was a friend," Asher said. "He lived in a flutter of pixies not far from my home mountain."

"You never told me that," Ladon said slowly. "I assumed you'd hired him."

"One less burden for you to carry. You were busy trying to hold a rebellion together and take down a corrupt dragon king without getting us all executed for treason."

Asher had carried this one alone. For them both.

"Gods damn it, Asher." The scowl that settled over his friend's face would've made him pause on a different day. Maybe.

"My choice."

"I don't give a shit," Ladon was snarling now. So damn rigid he might as well be carved from the very mountain itself.

"It's history," Asher pointed out. "Over."

It didn't exactly help.

"Tell me now." Another command.

Except Asher was done packing. He swung the bag over his shoulder and the room pitched sideways, but sheer stomach-lurching grit righted it after a second. "He was my best friend. His family were like a second family to me."

"Were?" Ladon asked. "And you think he died because of you?"

Asher shook his head. "There's a reason I couldn't tell his family, including Gwen. She's his sister. I can't tell you either."

A blood vow covered not being able to disclose that one had ever been made. Pixie magic was that thorough. And Goran had known that.

"Sister," Ladon tasted the word. The implications. "The pixie who is your fated mate?"

Asher nodded.

Ladon's eyes suddenly narrowed. "You knew *then* she was fated and still didn't tell her?"

"I...knew she was special to me." But not more than that.

It'd been just a whisper in his mind. Easily shaken off as wishful thinking. Asher took a deep, steadying breath. "But I'm sure now. And I couldn't tell her then, Ladon."

Hells, even saying this much was a risk.

He had no fucking clue how he was going to get around the blood oath, but he was going to damn well try. Or die with the truth on his lips.

Either way, he had to end this.

His king jerked his gaze away, looking at the blank rock wall of Asher's bedroom, but no doubt thinking through the past, what had just happened in Indonesia, and what all it meant to Asher.

He clasped his hands behind his back, his gaze back on Asher and dead serious.

"I will not accept your resignation…yet."

"Ladon—"

His king held up a head. "You're on leave for as long as it takes you to do what you need to. Then discuss it with your mate. If she agrees you should resign, I'll accept it, but she has a home here, too. Tell her that first."

Asher's chest clenched around emotions he couldn't deal with now. All he could do was swallow around the lump in his throat and nod.

Ladon stepped to the side, clearing the way out of the room. "Go get her."

CHAPTER NINETEEN

Gwen

This was the place a spirit pixie lived?

Gwen didn't have a clear expectation in her head, but it wasn't this.

This wasn't…scary enough.

Based on what her mother had said and her father's reaction to Gwen choosing to come here, she'd expected giant spiders maybe, or a hellhound, at least one banshee. She cast her gaze over what, at first glance, looked like a large boulder, but to a pixie was so obviously a massive, petrified snail shell with a small, arched door, a few tiny windows, and a chimney pipe popping out of the top, white smoke wisping out of the top.

The wooden door sat slightly askew in the frame. But it couldn't be where desperate pixies came to commune with their dead. Could it? This looked too…cozy.

Are we even in the right place?

She glanced over her shoulder at her mother. Tall and slender, with similar coloring to Gwen's, Mauren Moonsoar had, at one point, been a Guardian, one of the pixies selected to protect their kind from the predators of the supernatural world. She'd seen horrors even Gwen, after all her time as a courier, couldn't imagine.

But right now, her mother stared at the little hovel with a face gone a little green, her lips pressed together in a flat line so that she looked like she was holding back words.

Was her mother regretting that decision?

After she'd learned that Asher was going to make a full recovery and ensured the eggs' safe delivery, Gwen had come home. Finally. She'd gone straight to her parents after leaving the green dragon mountain in China. Then she'd told them everything. From start to finish. Well…save for a few key details that involved a certain dream situation. But it wasn't until she shared her suspicion that she and Asher were fated mates that her mother had reluctantly offered this solution.

A dangerous one.

Her father, furious at his wife for making the suggestion at all, had tried to talk Gwen out of it. He'd told her that a visit to a spirit pixie resulted in death or insanity more often than anything else, and those who did emerge with their lives and minds intact often regretted going. Maybe the dead usually didn't have good news to impart.

Made sense. Visiting the dead seemed like it would probably involve regrets and things left unfinished or unsaid. Not always kind things.

Her father had locked himself in his room when he'd failed to convince her not to come here, and refused to see her off.

Mamie had insisted on coming with her.

That both her parents feared losing another child was obvious.

I hate putting them through this.

But she wasn't here for regrets. Not really. Just truth.

I'll be okay. Goran would never hurt me.

"Mamie?" Gwen asked. "Are we here?"

Mauren flicked her gaze around them, like she was checking for danger, then gave a sharp nod.

"Do I just…knock?" Like they were here for a cup of tea and a friendly chat?

"I don't know what happens next," her mother said.

Gwen's stomach turned a little sour. Her mother was never short on answers. She knew everything, but not this?

Gwen went to step toward the hovel, but her mother's hand on her arm stayed her, and suddenly she found herself wrapped up in her mother's tight embrace. "Love and family wait for you on the other side, darlin.' Remember that?"

"You're not coming with me?"

Her mother shook her head. "I can't. Only one person for each of the dead. Ever."

Only one.

Gwen would be the only person from her family to see Goran's face again. Hear his voice.

Maybe.

She swallowed. "Are you sure you don't want to be the one—"

Mamie squeezed her tighter. "I promised myself the day Goran died that I would not cave to the urge to see him in death. I think, for me at least, the pain of seeing him again, only to lose him once more, would be too much. He wouldn't want that for me or your father."

Goran probably wouldn't want that for her either.

Mamie loosened her arms, then turned Gwen toward the hovel and gave her a gentle push. "Be brave. Listen to the elder. Do only what she tells you to."

Right.

Heart banging around in her chest, Gwen knocked on the door, then hesitated as it swung open of its own accord with a rusty creak and scraping over the stone floor.

Stop letting your imagination run off. Just take each step as it comes.

Not wanting to trespass, she leaned forward, looking around. The inside matched the outside. Cozy furniture. A tea pot warming on top of an ancient aga. A table where a meal was halfway eaten, recently as it looked fresh.

But no living creature.

"Elder Spiritwhisper?" she called out tentatively.

She hadn't even known of the pixie who lived here, despite the elder living close to Gwen's home flutter. Granted, on the very outskirts of the protected, magically warded borders, and apparently, she kept to herself for centuries at a time. A loner.

Probably for good reason.

"A visitor!" A tiny, shaky voice sounded from beside her. Squeaked really. "How lovely. It's been ages."

Gwen whirled around to find her mother gone. In her place stood a pixie maybe half Gwen's size in height, with long, wispy hair so white it might as well be translucent. The hair made the shock of her eyes—black as pitch but filled with starlight—even more profound.

Those dark eyes went a little hazy as she glanced over Gwen's right shoulder like she was looking at...something. "Of course it's lovely. Even kittens get lonely."

What? Kittens?

"Guests are not the demon's tools," the elder said next, clucking her tongue as she continued to address the spot over Gwen's shoulder.

Gwen turned slightly. Was someone in there she hadn't seen?

But no. Nothing was behind her. The one room home appeared empty to her.

"Come along, Gwendolyn Moonsoar."

Gwen leaned back a little. *She knows my name?*

The elderly pixie flitted past Gwen into her home. Gwen hesitated at the threshold.

"Come or go, but don't leave the door open," she was told.

Okay.

Gathering her courage like moonlight, Gwen stepped into the dark interior of the room. The interior was brightened only by small windows, a roaring fire in a massive stone fireplace, and candles everywhere dripping wax onto the tables in gloops and globs.

The elder set down a basket of flowers and herbs on the table. "A stitch in time," she mumbled, then nodded and hummed to herself as if someone had answered.

Gwen glanced around, the fine hairs on her neck raising. They weren't alone. She could feel that now. Did the elder see spirits all the time?

"Um…I'm here to request—"

"Goran's been waiting for you, m'dear." The elder sat in one of the three chairs at the table, the one not set before the food, and patted another empty seat to her right. Gwen guessed she was leaving the food for…whatever else was in the room with them? Did spirits eat?

Focus, Gwen. Do everything she says and nothing more.

Taking a shaky seat, Gwen swallowed. "You know my brother?"

"Fish and fair meet afoul," the tiny pixie answered in a singsongy voice, then her eyes seemed to clear a bit. "Goran visits from time to time. He hoped you would come, eventually."

Me?

"Why?" the word barely escaped her stiff lips.

"He has atonements to make." The elder furrowed her brow. "No. Not atonements. He needs to fix something." She glanced at the chair before the food. "I talk to him. You don't." A beat, then, "Oh, be quiet, do."

Gwen glanced between the pixie and the empty chair. "May I... I hate to ask but..."

Before she could get out the rest of her request, the elder leaned forward and blew out the candle on the table. Impossibly, the entire room went as dark as a cave, every single fire and candle out, but the windows also...gone.

It was the kind of dark that could spread through you like the poison from a wraith, but Gwen was a moon pixie. She lived in the darkness in order to find her light.

Seven hells, she *brought* her own light.

To her, this dark wasn't malicious. Not like when the wraiths had come for them. This was a comforting sort of warmth that held you and whispered to trust, but also to be brave.

Brave.

Her mother had told her that, with a face pinched with worry. To be brave.

"No matter what happens—" The elder's voice sounded all around her, like they were in a hollow cave. "Do not look at me and do not leave your seat. Understand?"

Stomach twisting, Gwen nodded. "Yes."

A new flame of a purer light ignited, and she found they were still at the same table, but with a different candle and no food or room around them. Just the table and chairs in a pool of impenetrable darkness. She couldn't even see the chair across from her.

Movement to her left, where the spirit pixie sat tried to draw her gaze, but Gwen stiffened her neck, refusing to look.

Elder said don't look. No matter what.

As if the candle was rewarding her for listening to

instructions, the flame grew taller, and the light moved outward, bringing the rest of the table and the other empty chair into view.

And in the chair sat Goran.

Gwen gasped, her hands flying up to cover her mouth. She had no idea what she'd expected, but it hadn't been this.

He looked…real. Solid, and healthy, and perfect.

And as young as he had been the last time she'd seen him.

"Goran," she croaked his name, tears stinging the backs of her eyes and clogging her throat. "Is it really you?"

He smiled, that crooked, goofy smile that was all his, his brown eyes warm. "Hi, Gwennie-penny."

For the first time in her entire life, she loved hearing that ridiculous nickname from him. Instinct and an overwhelming need to hug her brother had her twitching to get up, only he jerked out a hand, fear crossing his features. "Don't move."

Oh. Right. Don't look left. Don't get out of the chair.

She forced herself to settle back, her gaze skating over features so dear her heart tumbled and soared and ached all at the same time, just at the sight of him. "Hi, Goran."

Seeming to relax a bit, like she'd passed another test, Goran's smile returned, even wider.

Gwen swallowed again. "I've missed you so much."

His expression didn't dim, exactly, but turned more peaceful and yet serious somehow. "Me, too. We don't have much time."

They didn't? Her heart lurched, sadness trying to creep into the moment and steal the joy of seeing his face away from her. If they didn't have much time, then…

"I need to ask you—"

"I already know." He waved her question aside. "Asher didn't betray me for his king. The plan was always to let his enemies kill me if we were caught."

CHAPTER TWENTY

Asher

The place looked the same.

Gwen and Goran's childhood home was a two-story building of stone, white on the outside with quaint windows and a chimney. It looked like many a Scottish cottage, but it was anything but what it seemed. The entire village where they lived was warded to appear human. Protected in all sorts of magical ways.

As a boy, he used to run right inside without knocking. Welcomed into the fold by voices calling his name or telling him where Goran and Gwen were. Offering to feed him. Telling him he'd grown even since the day before.

The last time he'd come, it had been with bad news.

Even his dragon, who'd been pushing so hard to get here, had tucked his tail and paused.

Facing Goran and Gwen's family again wasn't going to be easy.

Asher hoped like hells they'd tell him if they knew which way Gwen had headed. Delilah already said that Gwen was on "sabbatical," and she didn't know where her pixie courier had gone.

Raising his hand, Asher knocked before nerves could make him rethink coming here.

Her family was his best bet at finding her fast.

If they cooperated—

The door swung open, and Asher found himself facing Ewen Woodshield. Gwen's father. Lean and tall for a pixie, he wasn't dragon-sized, and yet he had always been slightly intimidating with a thick black beard now greying around the mouth.

He took one look at Asher, blinked, then anger filled his eyes in a blazing scowl.

Faster than Asher had ever seen a pixie move, Ewen raised both his hands, his wings suddenly appearing, and before Asher could so much as take a step back, roots and vines exploded from the woods surrounding their home. They shot right at him, wrapping around him like a hundred snakes, pinning his arms to his sides.

Then the vines dragged him off into the woods.

Panic threatened worse things than the vines, his heart thudding painfully with it. Asher held onto his control with an iron fist as, with a complete disregard for the racket they were making, Ewen hauled him between trees and over boulders and brooks, and yet he didn't hit a single rock or tree. Thank the gods. He wasn't back to full strength after the wraith's poison yet.

Suddenly, the vines yanked him off the ground to dangle him upside down in the air.

Asher didn't struggle to free himself. Instead, he waited, watching, searching the forest around him. At the same time, he tried to slow his beating heart, and the stab of truth that these people who'd once loved him didn't trust him anymore. To this extent.

So many things to fix.

They came from overhead, Ewen...and all of Gwen's siblings... stirring the air with the flutters of their wings.

Woodshields.

Unlike Gwen's and Mauren's, the coloring of their wings were all about browns and greens and greys, in hues that could look dull one second and then catch the light just right during another, turning to something brighter.

Ewen landed in front of where Asher dangled, and behind their father, her siblings lined up. All of them. Arms crossed, faces rigid with anger.

He would never fight Gwen's family. He'd given them space after Goran had died, knowing that all he was to them was a painful reminder. But this...

They'd been keeping this from him.

Their blame.

Like having pieces of flesh sliced off him with a thousand sharp-bladed knives.

His fire would make short work of the wooden lashings holding him captive. But the fear in their eyes...that was what kept him still, waiting for whatever came next.

"Where is she?" he asked.

Her father's jaw hardened. "You don't get to demand things of us."

Not an answer.

"Ewen—"

"No." Ewen slashed a hand through the air. And that's when Asher saw it. The fear in Gwen's father's eyes.

Not fear of Asher. This was different. This was... was Ewen afraid *for* Gwen?

"If she's in danger, tell me," he said, holding onto a growing panic clawing at his own belly. "I can help her."

Ewen stared at him in silence, a muscle ticking at the side of his mouth.

"Please," Asher begged. He stared them down from his rather awkward viewpoint…and waited for the answer.

"Tell him, Da,'" Garrett, the youngest of the family spat the words. "He deserves to know what he's done to her."

The bindings groaned in protest as Asher's entire body went stiff. "What does that mean? Done to her?"

Ewen Woodshield crossed his arms, his face set, though more fear crept through the cracks. "Mauren took her to the spirit pixie."

Spirit pixie.

Okay.

"What does that mean?"

"Gwen has gone to speak to the dead."

Speak to the—

The blood drained from his head, quite a feat in his current position. The effect must've been pretty damn obvious, because for a second, the hardness disappeared from Ewen's expression, a frown or maybe confusion flickering there instead. Several of Gwen's siblings glanced at each other.

"Goran?" Asher asked, his voice a harsh tear. "She's gone to speak to Goran."

"She said she has to hear the truth from him," Garrett snapped. "*You* did this to her. You wouldn't tell her what happened, so she's gone to find out."

I can't. Asher didn't say it. He only had one shot to convince someone before the oath took him, and that had to be Gwen.

Her family wouldn't be this upset if this spirit pixie thing wasn't serious. "Is it dangerous?"

They didn't need to answer. He could see it in the strain on their faces, in their tightly held bodies.

His own fear rose up like those fucking wraiths, trying to drag him to his death.

Save her. Now.

He wasn't sure if that was his thought, or his dragon's.

"Returning to us with her mind intact will be a miracle," Ewen said, every word a poisoned arrow to Asher's heart. "If she comes back at all."

Fuck.

"Release me," Asher thrashed in his bindings.

Ladon would be proud. He'd sounded like a king.

"What if you make it worse?"

They would never trust him. Not after Goran. Not until they knew the truth. But he'd never risk Gwen for them to find that out. He had to get to her. Now.

Screw this.

Asher sucked in hard, stoking the fire in his belly, desperation snarling through him, driving him. Without shifting, blue fire erupted from his mouth, eviscerating the woody bindings around his body, reflecting in the shocked eyes of Gwen's family.

"I love her," he said as the last binding dropped away and he fell to the ground in a heap. "I'll stop her."

They stared at him with hard faces and hard eyes, Ewen in particular, his gaze…assessing. Measuring.

"I'm only allowing it because it's what Gwen would want."

Another turn of the knife in his heart, but Gwen was what mattered most right now. "Where?"

Her father pointed. "That way."

Asher jumped to his feet and took off at a dead sprint.

CHAPTER TWENTY-ONE

GWEN

Shock was a thunderclap that had Gwen straightening so violently she slammed into the back of her chair.

They'd what?

They'd *planned* to let Asher's enemies kill Goran?

She couldn't even comprehend the words.

"What?" her voice wavered, and she took a deep breath. "Why in the seven hells would you do that?"

"Because I was already dying."

She didn't think anything could trump that first thunderclap, but this one did, reverberating through her bones. Gwen shook her head. Hard. And caught the tiniest glimpse of writhing in the dark off to her left.

Gluing her gaze to her brother, she shook her head again. "No. You were—"

"I carried the black death."

The black death.

Oh my gods. Tell me it's not true.

The phrase meant something much different to pixies than it did to humans. Her people associated the term with the only disease known to be both deadly and untreatable among their people. A horrific end where the infected would start to lose weight rapidly, turning almost skeletal before their wings and then their skin started to turn black, then liquify like something out of a horror movie. A rare but fatal illness.

None of her people had been able to determine the source, but it never struck multiple pixies in the same dwelling or flutter.

Goran had been infected with the black death?

When?

How?

Gwen curled in on herself, having to put her hands on the table to stay in her chair. This was a million times worse than she ever could imagine. How could the gods be so cruel?

No time.

She had no time to work through this new knowledge. She'd have to do that later. Dragging her head up, she looked at her brother.

He seemed beautifully at peace now, at least.

Rather than asking or denying any more, she simply said, "Tell me everything."

"When I started to show the signs, I came here to the elder and she confirmed it. I didn't tell anyone, because I had no intention of forcing our family to endure watching me die that way. I couldn't do that to any of you. I also had no intention of waiting for the end to catch up with me. So when Asher told me about his mission, I volunteered to help him."

Sounded exactly like Goran.

"I told him, after first binding him with a blood vow, that he could never tell anyone else."

Her brother had told Asher. Asher had known all along. And couldn't say anything.

A blood vow meant his death if he did.

Gwen was tempted to clamp her hands over her ears and not hear any more. But she'd come this far. She had to know.

"I also made him promise that if either of us was ever caught, I would take the blame and the death that was the obvious punishment for spying on the dragon shifters. It was the perfect way to prove his loyalty."

By killing his best friend?

"Because you were dying anyway." Her voice was a harsh whisper, ragged in her throat.

Goran nodded. All the answer she needed. "I wanted to leave this world on my own terms."

Gwen raised shaking hands to cover her mouth, rocking slightly. "You must have felt so alone. We could have been there for you—"

"Watching the people I love suffer would have made it worse for me."

She squeezed her eyes shut. "But that's what family does for each other, Goran."

"I know."

"You robbed us of the chance to be at your side, to love you through it..." She had to swallow back a sob, barely managing to keep it together. She forced her eyes open. "To say...goodbye."

Goran reached across the table like he wanted to take Gwen's hand, but at a movement to her left, he stopped. Her brother's expression twisted, emotions flitting across his features in rapid succession, so many she could feel them like her own, but especially the sadness. "I...regretted it after," he said. "Asher didn't know what he was swearing to. He trusted me. And after I was gone, I couldn't fix it."

And I made it worse. I abandoned Asher. Blamed him. Ran from him. We all did.

She'd never hated him, though, even when she tried to make herself.

Goran drew a long, shuddering breath, like the weight of this regret had been on him all this time. "I messed up a lot of things." He grimaced. "He lost part of his tail spike because of me."

That's when that had happened? How? She'd seen Asher directly after Goran's death. He hadn't appeared injured.

"I hurt him badly."

Badly had to be a mild term for it. It would have had to be catastrophic to be permanent. Asher shouldn't have even been walking when she saw him afterward.

Gods above. What else did I miss?

"I didn't realize the cost of my choices until I died and watched him struggle with how the blood oath meant hiding things from people he loved and taking the blame for my death." Goran leaned forward, intent. "He would have saved me, Gwen. You know that deep down."

She wanted to look away. To take a moment to absorb all this. But she couldn't and they were running out of time. "It never made any sense, but he wouldn't tell me the truth."

"Because of me." Goran's expression pinched. "Because he couldn't."

"Oh, Goran," she whispered.

"Tell him I release him. Tell him I'm sorry I ever put him in that position."

Gwen's ribs moved with a long inhale. Asher would probably feel the oath lift, but she nodded anyway. "I will."

"And I'm sorry to you, too," Goran whispered. "For keeping you and Asher apart. For not seeing what was right in front of me. Tell Mom and Dad the truth and the others, too. Tell them I hope they can forgive me."

She looked at Goran. "Other than this regret, are you... okay?"

His smile was more than she deserved. The warmth. The contentment. "I'm more than fine, Gwen. Tell them and I'll be able to rest finally."

Her eyes stung hard with tears, but she blinked them back, not wanting to miss a second of being able to see his face. "I will. I'll tell them."

After a second, he nodded.

The candle on the table flickered. Just a little. Growing dimmer, bringing the shadows in closer.

"Time's up, my lovelies," the elder sing-songed.

"How long do we have?" Gwen didn't know who she was asking.

"Seconds," Goran said. He leaned forward, already starting to sort of...fade away. His voice turned echoey, like he was calling down a long corridor. "I love you. I love our family."

"We love you too," Gwen choked, staring at her brother's beautiful face, trying to commit it to memory.

The candle went out, pitching her into total, obliterating darkness again.

Only this time, she was too overwhelmed to be afraid. Emotions battered her from every side, and she had no idea which to respond to first.

When the elder lit the candle again with a regular match, this time it was normal, yellowish light and they were back in the cozy, cluttered room with the food on the table.

The elder sighed in what sounded like deep content. "That boy didn't know how to quit," she said. "Visiting me all the time. Trying to get me to come to you, but that's not how it works. He knows that." The small face drew into a smile. "He'll be at peace now."

"I hope so," Gwen whispered.

"You'll miss him," the elder said to the chair, paused, then quieter, "Yes. I will, too."

Gwen hardly noticed. Her heart ached in ways so raw, and yet, it was already healed thanks to time. She wasn't sure if she wanted to cry or laugh or just smile, sitting with her brother's ghost. She could still feel him. Like the way it felt when he'd sleep in her room whenever she'd had nightmares as a little girl. Even if she kept her eyes closed, she knew he was there for her.

"Thank you," Gwen whispered.

The elder smiled in a way that was pure sunshine on her face. "This was one of the happier ones," she said.

Gwen didn't want to know what the sad ones must be like. "If I can ever do anything for you…"

The elder waved her off. "A visit every so often would be nice, but this is my gift. I was meant for this."

The same way Gwen was meant to wield magic with moonlight. She nodded her understanding as she pushed back from the table.

"Don't get up," she told the elder.

Then she felt compelled to lean down and kiss the papery skin of the very ancient cheek, receiving a tickled chuckle in return.

"Thank you again."

She got a light swat on her shoulder, followed by, "Get on wi' ya. Your mate is coming for you."

Gwen straightened abruptly. "So I was right? He's my mate?"

"The dragon shifter Goran was talking about? Yes. You two are fated."

Gwen had already suspected, but having it confirmed this way… Revelation usually came with a bang, but today Gwen learned it could come with a soft sort of acceptance. Like a sigh.

Maybe she'd always known.

Happiness filled up the holes inside her, like a stream filling up a pond before overflowing and running down to the next and filling it up too. Warm and perfect and radiant.

She ran for the door, but paused, glancing over the shoulder. "I'll come visit," she called back before she flung the door open and shot out of the tiny home.

Straight into Asher's arms.

CHAPTER TWENTY-TWO

ASHER

Instinct had Asher wrapping his arms around Gwen the moment she collided with him. That he'd found her at all had him closing them tighter around her.

He glanced over her head at Mauren, who he'd found pacing the hills staring in the direction of...nothing. Just more hills.

Ewen and all Gwen's siblings were hard on his heels.

They all stood now with various expressions of shock, worry, and blame, but also...maybe acceptance.

That part was good.

It was because of his own relief that he was keeping his shit together. Especially after the odd sensation like an ice pick being drilled through his hand, followed by something like what having a poltergeist drawn out of his skin might feel like.

By some miracle, she was in his arms. He wasn't letting

her go. Not this time.

Instead of pushing him away or stepping back, her arms circled round his back, and she buried her face in his chest.

Confusion collided with a second wave of relief and determination, leaving Asher swaying like he had after waking up from the wraith poisoning.

"Gwen?" he asked.

No response, but she didn't try to leave him.

Asher inhaled sharply. "Gwen, I came here for a reason." The words rushed out of him. Like if he could say it fast enough, maybe... "I should have gone after you years ago, but I was a coward. Instead, I hunkered down, convincing myself that living in my own personal hell was better for you. But I can't do that anymore. And I have something to tell you, and after I do, I don't want you to hurt anymore—"

Movement in the doorway of the small mountainside dwelling Gwen had burst from—one that hadn't been there a second ago—had him glancing over her head to see an elder pixie in the doorway gazing at him with deceptively young eyes in a wizened face that seemed to hold secrets in their twinkling black depths.

She smiled softly and closed the door.

"I'm sorry," Gwen murmured into his chest, still holding him tight.

What?

He tried to take her by the shoulders and pull her away just enough to see her face, but at the slightest hint of distance between their bodies, she surged back against him.

She's not running.

That's all he cared about. Turning his back on her family, and the pixie in the hut, he focused solely on her. Asher held her close, bringing one hand up to cradle the back of her head. "Sorry about what?" he asked softly.

She didn't speak for a long moment, and he just held her, and waited, trying not to worry.

"Asher?" she asked, in a small voice.

He hummed in response.

"I am a stubborn fool."

A statement that had him trying to see her face again, but she clung on tightly, so he went back to just holding her.

"I blamed you all this time," she said.

His heart flipped a little, not expecting that.

"Being away from you…these have been the worst years of my life. Like I was missing an important part of…me. I did that to us."

He shook his head. "You didn't. I—"

"I've loved you since I was a girl."

Her confession cut him off short.

"I never told you that," she said.

A small smile tugged at the corners of his mouth. At least he'd have this moment before he broke his blood vow and gave up his life. He could take this into the afterlife with him.

"And I knew…I knew deep inside that no matter what it looked like, that even though there wasn't any other explanation, that you would have saved Goran if you could. But you wouldn't *tell* me."

Asher squeezed his eyes shut. "I couldn't. I—"

"Goran told me," she said. And his heart stopped entirely. "Everything."

This time when he took her by the shoulders, she let him, looking into his eyes, hers clear and true, shimmering gold, and yet shadowed at the same time.

Vaguely he was aware of a murmur of noise behind them. Her family.

"I don't understand," he said.

She waved at the small house. "Goran told me. About the black death."

"What?" a wavering yelp sounded from Mauren behind them.

Gwen shot them a pained look, but then returned her gaze to him. "Goran wants me to tell you he was sorry. That he absolves you from the oath. That he made a mistake, not realizing the consequences."

Asher closed his eyes, picturing his friend's face. Not the day Goran died, but before then, when he'd been so vital, a prankster who loved to laugh.

Thank you, my friend. Rest now.

He sent the thought into the universe and hoped Goran heard.

Gwen laid her head on his chest, tightening her arms around him. "There's more…"

He rested his chin on the top of her head. "Tell me."

"I never want to leave you again."

Every piece of Asher, from his heart to his bones to his soul, stilled. As if he needed utter quiet so he didn't miss a single breath of hers.

Words he'd missed with an indescribable, heavy ache every day since the day he'd lost her.

"I love you, and I want us to be together," she said.

He smiled into her hair. Hell, he couldn't have stopped himself, happiness filling him up so high and fast he might as well be flying.

Thank the gods.

"Did you hear me?" Gwen pulled back slightly, looking up as he tipped his chin to look down at her.

To take in the beauty of her face. The hope and worry in eyes that searched his. Eyes that no longer aimed hurt and blame his way.

Gods, he loved this woman.

"Asher?"

He swooped, kissing her lips, claiming her as his.

After a surprised little gasp, Gwen sighed and melted into him. Neither of them gave their audience a second thought. They'd face all those truths soon enough, no doubt a poignant, difficult conversation, but everything was going to be okay. He knew that now.

This though…this moment was for them.

Asher raised his head. "I love you, too."

Then he swooped again and held Gwen tightly as he kissed her over and over. Not because she was going to run, but because she'd come home.

To him.

CHAPTER TWENTY-THREE

Gwen

Traveling on the back of a dragon was a hell of a lot faster than a pixie could fly. Hell of a lot windier too. And in Scotland, even in the summer, at altitude, it was damn cold. But Asher took care of that, stoking the fire inside him to warm her.

"Almost there," he let her know.

There.

He meant home.

Their new home.

After all the hard truths had been shared, and mourned, and regretted, and forgiven with her family, Asher had given her choices.

All choices that ended with them together.

He'd told her about attempting to resign from his position under the blue dragon king to come find her, and the king's offer for them to make their home here. In the end, she'd agreed that the best place for them was Ben Nevis, with Asher doing what he had been blessed with the skills to do best. The lovely part was how close in proximity they were to her own family. After them both being gone for so long, she knew they'd be spending a lot of time there.

Catching up.

They may have lost Goran, but the inevitability of that, and the way he'd chosen to leave this mortal coil, had somehow felt…better…than what they'd thought had happened. Maybe because Goran had been gone long enough that they'd already mourned losing him. Or maybe because they could welcome Asher back into their fold with loving arms.

Asher tipped his wings, spiraling down into treeless mountains then further, into a canyon she'd been able to see, but only because she was supernatural herself. Halfway to a river that wound itself between the crags, Asher dipped, then turned, flying straight through a huge opening into an even more massive hangar.

One full of people and dragons, who all turned to look, as Asher flared his wings wide, setting them down with a rocking motion. Rather than climb down, Gwen spread her fully restored wings, thanks to the healer pixie in their flutter, and flew to the ground.

A pixie's hearing wasn't nearly as sharp as a dragon's, but she still couldn't miss the hushed whispers that ran through the shifters gathered in the space.

"A pixie," they said. "Asher brought us a pixie."

Asher shifted back to his human form and joined her, slipping his hand into hers with a barely there smile just for her.

"Are you here for good, or just come for your belongings?" a rough, male voice called out.

They both turned to find Ladon and Skylar Ormarr

bearing down on them, trailing a large entourage of dragon shifters in their wake. Ones who exchanged glances.

Asher's hand around hers tightened, and then he was pulling her quickly toward Ladon and Skylar at first. The queen nodded at Gwen, who nodded back. She'd already met them after saving Asher and safely delivering the egg to Meilin together.

Only as they drew closer to the king and queen, Asher simply said, "We're staying, but introductions and niceties come later."

He said this without pausing in his rapid walking, practically dragging Gwen past the group who watched them disappear with a combination of surprise, curiosity, and smirking knowledge.

Which would have been hilarious if it wasn't directed her way on her first day in the mountain where she'd live the rest of her life. Heat flamed through her face.

"What are you doing?" she whisper-hissed at Asher.

He grunted.

Gwen grinned, but still squeezed his hand. "More information please."

"If you think we should stick around and make nice when there are more important things to be doing, then we really need to talk about your priorities."

His meaning couldn't have been any clearer…or spoken any louder. The heat in her cheeks flared all over her body.

Luckily, that's about when they passed into a blessedly empty tunnel that took them deeper into the mountain.

They emerged into a much larger cavern, and Gwen stopped dead as the hall opened up into what she could only call an atrium. The place was massive. Essentially, the mountain itself had been gouged out from the base to the top like a cone.

The ground level, where they stood, reminded Gwen of a

busy downtown street in any human city, except round. "Buildings" lined the rim, the faces built into the rock itself and taking up maybe two stories. The floors above that point appeared to be suites and rose up to the top of the cone. Under every balcony a giant slab of rock jutted out. Dragons flew overhead circling up to land on a perch where they'd shift, then walk inside.

"Wow," she whispered.

Asher, used to the place, took her pausing to stare as a chance to shift again. "Follow me, love."

Love. He'd started calling her that again, and it sent a shiver of delight through her every time. She hoped it never got old.

Unfurling her wings, she followed her dragon as he launched into the air. He flew up and up until he slowed and landed on one of the slabs, shifting quickly to walk down its wide balance-beam length and hop onto the balcony floor. Gwen landed beside him only to immediately be tugged into his embrace, his mouth on hers.

Hungry. Impatient. Driven.

Immediate need consumed her—sparkling and building— condensing in her core, molten and raw, stoked by fires that had been left as embers for far too long.

Asher devoured her and she gasped into every kiss, every touch, every growl in his throat, turned on even more when he pinned her to the wall, pressing into her, taking her hands to hold them captive above her head.

Gods, he felt good.

This felt so...

He yanked her away from the wall, spinning them and using one hand to pull her arms around his neck.

Clinging to him, turning hazier and more flushed with every kiss, unconsciously Gwen started to tuck her wings away.

"No," he said roughly. "Leave them out."

Her belly turned squishy at the simple knowledge of why he was asking her that. A pixie's wings weren't like a butterfly's, which were ruined if you touched them. Instead, their wings were an erogenous zone.

And Asher knew that.

"At least let me get my top off," she murmured against lips that wouldn't leave hers.

"Mm-hmm," he growled.

Still kissing him, Gwen tucked her wings away and, with his own hands right there to help, tugged her shirt over her head.

They did this as he walked her backward through some kind of apartment that she wasn't paying the slightest bit of attention to. Her clothes, his, all came off in a rush, until they were standing in a bedroom, breathing heavy, and stark naked, except for her wings, which she unfurled again.

She expected him to go straight for her breasts, which were a nice handful, she'd always thought. Not large, but not small, and nicely pert.

But he didn't.

Instead, he took her face in his hands, indigo eyes suddenly darker both with need, and now with serious intent.

"If we mate…"

"Not if," she interrupted.

He grimaced. "Please, love. I have to say this."

She covered his hands with hers and smiled. "I'm listening."

"If we mate, you might turn dragon."

That's what he was worried about?

"If the elder pixie was wrong, and we're not fated, I'll die. Isn't that more of a—"

Asher shook his head. "That no longer happens to our

mates. Not since the phoenix rose to power. Her magic has… changed things. If we choose each other, you won't die."

A tiny, huffed laugh escaped from her. "Well, that's nice."

She'd been holding onto the worry ever since they'd decided to be together again. Pixies lived not quite as long as dragons, but close. And she was younger than Asher, in terms of years. So if they couldn't truly mate, they'd still be mates in her heart and together for centuries to come.

That could have been enough.

Maybe.

But knowing they could safely join themselves now, in a way so fundamental, so primal? Her heart tripped over itself in joy.

"That's good."

He didn't smile. "I won't take who you are away from you."

She smiled for him. Radiant with it, she could feel the love pouring from her. "You won't."

His brows drew together in a quick frown.

"My mother pulled me aside before we left and explained how it works when dragons mate other supernatural creatures. It's not the dominant power that wins out. It's a choice. *My* choice."

Asher's shoulder dropped. "Thank fuck for that."

Gods, she loved this man to the depths of her soul.

Knowing he would have stopped. Knowing he would have given up the extra years that being mated gifted dragons just to be with her.

It meant everything.

And then all rational thought deserted her as Asher claimed her lips once more, urgent and yet reverent. The difference was subtle, but she felt it with each brush, each sweet swipe of his tongue, the way they clung together.

His hands dropped from her face, tracing the contours of

her body, brushing over a ripe breast, circling her nipple in teasing swirls before cupping her, testing the weight, then down over the gentle slopes of her belly, passing the thatch of soft hair at the juncture of her thighs to trace her hips. To grip them tightly, urging her back on the bed.

"I've dreamed of this," he murmured against her lips, before trailing them down her neck. "Touching you like this. Having you in my bed, in my arms."

The burn of tears in her eyes was welcome now. Bittersweet. The time they'd lost was gone forever, but they still had so much more ahead of them.

She refused to look back. Only forward.

And forward were years filled with joy, and laughter, and sharing, and more of this.

Asher ran one hand from the point at the top of her wing down the edge, and Gwen arched into him as pure need shot through her, turning her slick. Ready.

She shuddered. "Don't stop...Keep doing that until you want me to come."

He lifted his head and watched her face as he did the same thing to the other side and she arched again, trembling by the time he finished, a molten mass of quivering need. She needed to find a release from the pleasure that had built fast and hard.

Asher grinned, his gaze taking in the flush of her face, the way her breasts rose and fell in time to her rapid breaths. "I plan to make you come often, love. I'll make up for all the pleasure you missed because of—"

Gwen put a finger to his lips. "No more blame. No more guilt. What happened...happened, and it was for reasons that involved love and loyalty, even if those reasons hurt us both. Now it's time to just be together. Okay?"

She felt the small puff of his breath against her finger a second before he pressed a kiss to the tip. "Okay."

He drew a circle with one finger around one of the golden spots on her wing, and Gwen shuddered again.

"But I'm still going to make you come over and over for me, love. Just for the fun of it."

Gwen's laugh turned into a moan as he did the same to a spot on her other wing.

From there things turned frantic as they both lost themselves in each other. Touching. Kissing. Nipping. Laughing. Moaning.

Asher built her to two climaxes, first by her wings alone, and then with his mouth on her body before he finally spread her out on the bed, pressing her legs wide as he entered her.

Her breath caught at the sensation of him inside her.

She'd dreamt of this. So many times.

And now it was real. The way he stretched her, filled her. Consumed her.

The way he moved so that he hit just the right spot with every slow, torturous stroke. The way he looked into her eyes as he thrust. As he claimed. As he built them both up, creating a storm of sensation in her. As they neared the precipice. Together.

"Open your mouth, my love," he said. "Accept my fire."

He placed his mouth over hers and a sound like a bellows in a forge rumbled from him, then a new warmth poured down her throat, spreading out through her chest, then lower, filling her from the inside as he pushed his fire into her.

The mating kiss of a dragon shifter.

"Eyes on me, Gwen," Asher growled, as he took both her hands to pin them above her head, lacing their fingers together, thrusting his hips, stoking that heat with every stroke.

Flames spread and flowed and consumed, driving the

sizzling sensations they'd already built together to the tipping point.

In the same instant, all that sensation sort of pulled in tight, gathering at the base of her spine, Asher swelled inside her, stretching her more.

"Come now, love," he commanded.

Gwen's entire body contracted into the feeling.

Asher kept his eyes on hers as he bore down and roared his own release, a powerful sound that dominated her soul, that matched her, echoing her own cries of pleasure. And a second fire entered her from the juncture at her thighs.

Holding on to Asher for dear life, she never looked away. Not even when yet another orgasm slammed through her body, matching his. He pounded into her body as he claimed her, made love to her, worshipped her. His fire burned into her and through her and out of her.

Scouring her.

Remaking her, she realized. Through ecstasy and burning.

And as they slowed, as she started to turn languorous and sated, as the last of his fire touched the outermost parts of her, she saw it.

In her mind's eye.

Two versions of herself. One as she was now—a moonlight pixie. The other as a blue dragoness. Pale, pale blue, similar to moonlight over water.

And for a second, she was tempted.

To be able to fly with her mate, play with him in that form. Fight at his side.

But she could never give up her heritage, her own magical powers, her connection to the moon. And Asher loved her exactly as she was.

So she chose.

And the burning sizzled away, leaving her gloriously,

beautifully, incandescently sated. She went to curl her arms around his neck. He was still seated deep inside her, and she had every intention of keeping him that way until they were both ready for another round.

He was right. They had some catching up to do. But wouldn't that be fun?

Only as she sleepily, blissfully reached for him, a sudden searing pain at the back of her neck brought her to gasping wakefulness.

It flared white hot, then died out just as quickly. Even so, she lifted her hand to the flesh at her nape, a tiny bit scared it would have been burned away.

But it hadn't.

In fact, her skin was cool to the touch, save a slightly puckered mark that she traced with her fingertips. Asher's family mark, linking her…his mate…to his line permanently.

Their bond snapped into place with ease, and then, as natural as breathing, she could *feel* him. Feel his essence, his being. And the utter happiness he sat with now.

"Let me see," he murmured. And she went up on her elbows, leaning and turning as much as she could without dislodging him.

The second he spotted his mark, he growled a possessive sound, and a wave of supremely male satisfaction flooded through her from their bond.

Gwen grinned. "I think you like—"

His cock swelled inside her, immediately as hard as it had been only moments ago.

"Like it," she breathed out. Her own body already heating, readying to meet him in their pleasure again.

Asher put his lips to the mark, *over* the mark, and sucked. Hard.

Hard enough to add a second mark to her skin. And as he did, he pumped his hips.

He lifted his head and growled in her ear, hips still thrusting. "I fucking love it…mate."

And grinning from ear to ear, Gwen held on for the ride.

For the start of their life together. No more separation. No more loneliness. No more isolation.

She was his.

Just as he was hers.

EPILOGUE

The modern penthouse that took up the entire floor of the New York skyscraper was understated in a way that made the wealth more obvious. Humans did so love to try to reach their gods, climbing their buildings ever higher into the skies.

Where they didn't fucking belong.

But the person standing at the floor to ceiling window, hands clasped behind their back, staring out at the sparkling city lights that drowned out the night stars here...they belonged up here.

"Your Worthiness," a silky-smooth voice sounded from the shadows in the room.

One of the army of wraiths they'd amassed.

They didn't turn. "Report."

"We did not retrieve the egg, I'm afraid."

The cowering in the wraith's tone could set one's teeth on edge.

"It is now with Luu Meilin."

The green dragon queen. The mountain that served as the green dragons' fortress base was as close to impenetrable as any place could get. Their wraiths would be useless against dragons. But wraiths weren't the only creatures they'd amassed into an army.

"We make our most humble apologies for this failure."

A bored hand waved that away. "How many did we lose?"

"Sixteen."

An unlucky number. That was unfortunate. "Dismissed."

The wraith disappeared with no sound, and yet the person still standing at the window could feel their retreat like a physical touch in the air.

The senses the gods had graced their kind with helped with that.

"The green dragon queen will be the key," the monster murmured.

Its smile was one of brutal anticipation.

Do you want to see more of Asher?

Keep reading for excerpts from both
The Mate (a Fire's Edge FREE prequel novella)
& The Rogue King (Inferno Rising book 1)...

EXCERPT FROM THE MATE

Did you know that Asher Kato first appeared in *The Mate*, the FREE prequel novella from my Fire's Edge dragon shifters series?

Here's a small peek at the first time we meet Asher on the page…

A few years before An Accident Waiting to Dragon,
just before the War of the Dragon Kings…

No way could Fallon watch his mate walk right to her death, but intervening would get him killed, too.

As Jagar talked, a man he hadn't noticed earlier made his way across the room to where Fallon stood propping up the doorway. With narrowed eyes, he considered the man's face, which seemed oddly familiar. Eyes a shade of dark blue they almost appeared black returned his stare.

"Asher Kato?" Fallon asked slowly, as recognition struck.

A nod confirmed it, and Fallon held out a hand, despite not feeling like being sociable right this moment.

Asher was one of the best fighters Fallon had ever seen. He'd almost been sent to the Huracáns about the time Finn had been assigned. Instead, Asher had been assigned to King Thanatos's personal guard, a position Fallon had been surprised Asher accepted. He'd been under the impression that the navy-colored dragon shifter was not a huge fan of the king, though Asher'd never said as much.

"What are you doing here?" Fallon asked.

"I've been sent as a temporary representative of the Blue Clan for this mating since we have a new blue dragon mate to welcome."

"You may be mourning a dead mate," Fallon muttered.

Asher lifted a single eyebrow.

Fallon kept his gaze away from Maddie. Looking at her hurt too much. He'd take distraction anywhere he could get it. Something about Asher's comment penetrated the numb haze settling over him. It seemed off, especially when paired with his earlier visit from Jagar and Macon. Fallon ran it through his mind again.

"Does this not happen often? A blue dragon mate?" he asked, low enough to fly under the hearing of the shifters in the room as their focus was turned elsewhere.

"Not lately," Asher affirmed, lips flat.

How was that possible?

Whatever color brand the dragon mate showed would dictate which clan was selected. No way would the Council risk the fallout by doing something questionable with the women who showed dragon sign. Sure, having a mate meant a longer life span, and even a bit more clout in the scheme of things, since they could provide more dragons to a clan, but the Mating Council had one representative for each clan here to keep things balanced.

Asher checked over his shoulder again, but no one was paying them any attention. "I'm also here to warn you and the others. Something is about to happen in our clan that could potentially cause problems if you're still here when it goes down."

What problems? "Can you tell me more?"

Asher twitched a shoulder. "Not yet."

Jagar's gaze passed over them, assessing.

Fallon raised his voice to a deliberate pitch to be overheard. "How long are you staying?"

Asher also raised his voice. "Only until the mating process is complete."

Jagar moved on.

"How long do I have?" Back to low murmurings.

"It's a fluid situation. A day, maybe two."

Shit. "Do I need to get Maddie out of here?"

Asher crossed his arms. "Will she go with you?"

Good fucking question. Not after she chose a different mate. No way could he let that happen. He'd risk exile to keep her safe and alive. A plan started to form in his head. "Keep me posted."

Asher tipped his chin toward the front of the room. "You're up."

🦇

READ THE MATE NOW!

THE MATE

A FREE FIRE'S EDGE PREQUEL NOVELLA

You've never met dragons quite like these...

Maddie Thompson's life just fell down a rabbit hole. Finding out she's a dragon shifter was one thing—she never quite fit into the human world, and this new reality feels...strangely right. However, discovering the next step is to choose a mate, and if she chooses wrong she'll die, is the other side of crazy. Especially when she already left a piece of her heart with someone who didn't want it.

To say dragon enforcer Fallon Conleth was shocked when the Mating Council summoned him as a potential mate for a newly found dragon doesn't quite cover it. A mate is rare and precious and many dragons never find theirs. Fallon isn't sure he's worthy of the honor, not when so many deserve it more. He'll just go through the motions and return home alone...until he sees Maddie. The human woman he reluctantly let walk away.

Fallon already broke Maddie's heart once, but if he can't convince her that they're meant to be, she'll die... and he won't be far behind.

READ *THE MATE* FOR FREE NOW!

EXCERPT FROM THE ROGUE KING

Did you know that Asher Kato is a featured secondary character in my Inferno Rising dragon shifters series?

Here's a small peek at when we meet Asher in book 1, *The Rogue King*...

A few years before An Accident Waiting to Dragon, just as the War of the Dragon Kings is heating up...

Brand tried not to see when the king placed a hand at Kasia's back, ushering her across the room. "I would like you to meet my men," Ladon said to her. "These are my personal guard, as well as my closest friends and fiercest warriors."

The men didn't make a sound, but they stood taller, shoulders back, heads held high—proud.

"Fallon you've already met," Ladon waved.

Fallon winked at her, eyes twinkling.

She nodded at the healer who'd helped her earlier in the day. The shortest of the group—which wasn't saying much, since he was still at least six feet tall—Brand didn't like the way he smiled so casually at Kasia. Wasn't the guy mated?

The next man was the one to keep an eye on, even among these hardened, skilled warriors.

"This is Asher," Ladon said. "He is my Beta as well as part of my Curia Regis, Viceroy of Security."

Asher nodded, and Kasia returned the gesture.

Ladon continued with the rest of the introductions, and most of the men nodded at Kasia, though some, like Reid and Asher, with more reserve than others.

Ladon took Kasia's hand, tugging her around to face him, and Brand clenched his fists at his sides at the simple touch from the other man. "As my personal guard," Ladon explained. "They will take turns guarding you as well now."

Kasia scowled and let go of his hand. "I don't need babysitters." She glanced at the men. "No offense."

The big bald one guffawed. "None taken."

Ladon wasn't backing down though. "We're under a constant state of attack. Mostly small skirmishes, and none have made it inside the mountain yet. However, I expect that to increase as word of a phoenix leaks out, and I'm not taking a chance with you."

Kasia crossed her arms. "Am I a prisoner?"

"Your Grace." The quiet correction came from Asher.

"Excuse me?" Kasia said with a tiny frown.

"He's your king. You address him as 'Your Grace,'" Asher clarified, expression not giving an inch.

Kasia snuck a quick glance at Brand, but he wasn't her protector anymore. Fists clenching harder until his nails digging into the flesh of his palms drew blood, he held still and said nothing.

So she turned back to Asher. "He's not my king. Not yet, at least."

Six glowers met those words. She definitely wasn't winning friends with that comment. Brand held his position by the door and did his damnedest not to put himself bodily between her and the angry shifters forming a wall in front of her.

If he could, he would've turned his back to them. Hell, if he could, he wouldn't be here in the first damn place, especially not after the way he'd helped her orgasm in her room. But Ladon had asked him to stand as Kasia's personal bodyguard, taking the majority of the shifts with her until the king mated her. The idea being he'd bond with Ladon's other most trusted warriors gradually.

Just his fucking luck she'd get herself in trouble within five minutes of meeting them. She'd have to get herself out of this, because he needed them on his side as much as she did. Maybe more.

Brand focused on his job. Physical protection only. But not too physical. Dammit. He scanned the people passing in front of the restaurant, but no one stood out. No alarm bells went off, which gave him plenty of time to listen in to the conversation going on inside the room.

Kasia sighed.

But rather than address his men, Kasia turned to Ladon and put a hand on his arm. The men tensed, Asher's hand going to the knife at his belt, the hiss of the metal against the scabbard audible.

Brand turned and loosed a warning rumble of noise, and the room went dead silent, tension thick enough to wring out of a wet towel blanketing all inside.

Fuckballs. Not his best move.

Ladon gave a single shake of his head, and the men eased

off. Sort of. Asher, at least, dropped the blade back into its holder. Brand, however, didn't relax. He waited.

Kasia slowly lowered her hand, clasping it behind her. "Can I be honest?"

Ladon regarded her unsmilingly. "Yes."

"Fancy isn't really my thing, and while I appreciate you trying to put me at ease at this lovely restaurant, introducing me to your…closest friends, I suspect fancy is maybe not your thing, either."

What the hell? Was that seriously what she wanted to say so earnestly?

Ladon stared at her for a beat, clearly as surprised as Brand, then laughed. A rusty, unused sound Brand had certainly never heard before. "That is definitely honest."

Even some of his warriors smiled, though not Asher.

Damn. Now Brand was going to have to keep an eye on that asshole.

READ *THE ROGUE KING* NOW!

Note: The Inferno Rising series will be re-released in trade paperback into stores with gorgeous brand new covers starting July 30, 2024!!!
PREORDER YOUR COPY NOW

THE ROGUE KING

INFERNO RISING BOOK 1

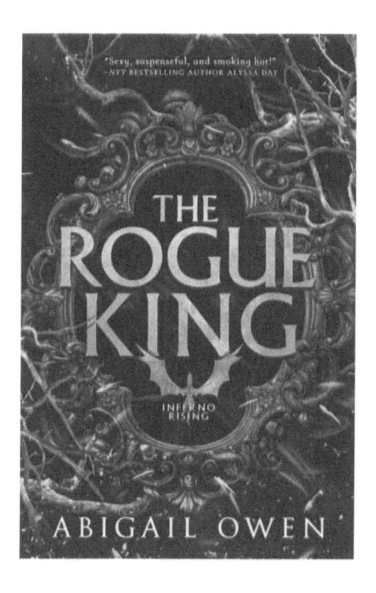

The burn of desire begins and ends in dragon fire.

Kasia Amon is a master at hiding. Who—and what—she is makes her a mark for the entire supernatural world. *Especially* dragon shifters. To them, she's treasure to be taken and claimed. A golden ticket to their highest throne. But she can't stop bursting into flames, and there's a sexy dragon shifter in town hunting for her…

As a rogue dragon, Brand Astarot has spent his life in the dark, shunned by his own kind, concealing his true identity. Only his dangerous reputation ensures his survival. Delivering a phoenix to the feared Blood King will bring him one step closer to the revenge he's waited centuries to take. No *way* is he letting the feisty beauty get away.

But when Kasia sparks a white-hot need in him that's impossible to ignore, Brand begins to form a new plan: claim her for himself… and take back his birthright.

READ *THE ROGUE KING* NOW!

Note: The Inferno Rising series will be re-released in trade paperback into stores with gorgeous brand new covers (featured above) starting July 30, 2024!!!

PREORDER YOUR COPY NOW

ALSO BY ABIGAIL OWEN

Don't miss the rest of Abigail's books...

For a suggested reading order,

go to Abigail's website…

abigailowen.com

ROMANTASY - NEW ADULT / UPPER YA

THE CRUCIBLE GAMES

THE GAMES GODS PLAY (coming Sept 3, 2024)

DOMINIONS

about to be completed trilogy

THE LIAR'S CROWN

THE STOLEN THRONE

THE SHADOWS RULE ALL (coming July 2, 2024)

PARANORMAL ROMANCE

INFERNO RISING

completed series

THE ROGUE KING

THE BLOOD KING
THE WARRIOR KING
THE CURSED KING

FIRE'S EDGE
completed series
set in the Inferno Rising world
THE MATE (free novella)
THE BOSS
THE ROOKIE
THE ENFORCER
THE PROTECTOR
THE TRAITOR

BRIMSTONE INC.
ongoing series of standalone stories
(no need to read in order)
set in the Inferno Rising & Fire's Edge world
THE DEMIGOD COMPLEX
SHIFT OUT OF LUCK
A GHOST OF A CHANCE
BAIT N' WITCH
TRY AS I SMITE
HIT BY THE CUPID STICK
AN ACCIDENT WAITING TO DRAGON

SHADOWCAT NATION
completed series
vintage titles / only available via Abbie's store
HANNAH'S FATE

ANDROMEDA'S FALL
SARAI'S FORTUNE
TIERYN'S FURY
SENECA'S FAITH

SVATURA

completed series

vintage titles / only available via Abbie's store

BLUE VIOLET
WHITE HYACINTH
CRIMSON DAHLIA
BLACK ORCHID

STANDALONE SHORT STORIES

THE WOLF I WANT FOR CHRISTMAS
PSYCHED

For a suggested reading order,

go to Abigail's website...

abigailowen.com

ABOUT THE AUTHOR

Award-winning author, Abigail Owen, writes New Adult/Upper YA romantasy and adult paranormal romance. She loves plots that move hot and fast, feisty heroines with sass, heroes with heart, a dash of snark, and oodles of HEAs!

Abbie has a degree in English Rhetoric (Technical Writing) from Texas A&M University (gig'em Ags!), and an MBA from California State University-Sacramento. Prior to becoming a published author, she spent 15+ years using the other side of her brain in various tech- and business-related roles.

Other titles include: wife, mother, Star Wars geek, ex-competitive skydiver, AuDHD, spreadsheet lover, Jeopardy fanatic, organizational guru, true classic movie buff, linguaphile, wishful world traveler, and chocoholic.

Abigail currently resides in Austin, Texas, with her own swoon-worthy hero, their (mostly) angelic teenagers, and two adorable fur babies.

Don't miss a new release and
get in on insider fun like bonus content,
early announcements, and all my giveaways…

Subscribe to my newsletter:
SUBSCRIBE

Follow me in all the places…

http://www.abigailowen.com

Abbie's Awesome Nerds
(Private Reader Facebook Group)

ACKNOWLEDGMENTS

Dear Reader,

I hope you loved Asher and Gwen's story! I've been wanting to give Asher his HEA ever since I mentioned the detail of his missing half his tail spike in *The Mate*, the prequel novella to my Fire's Edge series that he pops up in. Of course I had to give him a partner who would give him a hell of a time winning her over. If you are new to my books...I hope you'll check out both the Fire's Edge and Inferno Rising series set in the same dragon shifter world!

Writing and publishing a book doesn't happen without the support and help from a host of incredible people.

To my fantastic readers... Thank you from the bottom of my heart for going on these journeys with me, for your kindness, your support, and generally being awesome. Also, I love to connect with my readers, so I hope you'll drop a line and say "Howdy" on any of my social media! Also, if you have a free sec, please think about leaving a review.

To my beta readers and editors for this one... Heather Howland, Kait Ballenger, Cate Ashton, and Nicole Flockton, your feedback made this a better story!

To my team of friends, sprinting partners, beta readers, critique partners, writing buddies, reviewers, and family (you know who you are)... I know I say this every time, but I mean it... Your friendships and feedback and support mean the world to me.

To my family...thank you for your love and support and

for teaching me to look at the world through eyes of love, hope, joy, faith, empathy, and adventure!

Finally, to my husband and kids…I love you with every part of my heart and soul.

Xoxo, Abigail Owen
abigailowen.com